"It has been for Rose Gordy an unsettled life and in spite of all the changes and challenges she's continued to do what she loves most... to write."

Kristy Villa, host of Lifetime TV's "The Balancing Act"

"...her stories seem to me to be intended to awaken controversy."

John Thiel, editor of Pablo Lennis, the longest running sci-fi fanzine in the world

For old time's sake —

Unsettled Lives

A Collection of Short Stories

by

Rose Gordy

Rose Gordy

Rose Words Books

ISBN-13: 978-1456420093
ISBN-10: 1456420097

Cover images and photos courtesy of SuperClusterMedia.com

Rosewords Books
www.Rosewords.com

To all those who live lives of "quiet desperation"

Table of Contents

PART III

Introduction

I wrote my first short story when I was in second grade all of seven years old. My Mother kept it in a scrapbook - the only story that has survived for decades. Considering that I entered a convent eleven years later, it is a rather significant tale.

The Story of the Blessed Mother

One day baby was in bed. Then she saw a light in her room; it was the Blessed Mother.
She said, "Little girl, why are you always in your bed?"
The little girl said, "My mother will not let me come out."
"Well," said the Blessed Mother, "where is your mother?"
"She went to the store."
"When will she be back?"
"I don't know."
Then the Blessed Mother went away.

Naturally, the unsettledness of the little girl at the end foreshadows my stories in this collection entitled "Unsettled Lives." What happens to Joey in the story "Joey and the Mass" when he's taken away from the Hermitage on the Lake? Does the man in love with the newswoman in "Lila, The Love of His Lonely Life" ever realize the difference between reality and fantasy? How long does the former monk in "Elusive Peace" stay with his problem wife? What will Penny's life be like after what her Daddy does at the end of her story? These are only a few of the ongoing questions readers of these stories might ponder afterwards.

Encounter my stories considering Rilke's sentiments from Letters to a Young Poet quoted on the following page.

Rose Gordy
January 2011

Letters to a Young Poet
Letter Three (23 April 1903)

Have patience with everything unresolved in your heart and try to love
the questions themselves as if they were locked rooms or books in a
very foreign tongue. Do not search for answers, which could not be
given to you now, because you would not be able to live them. And the
point is to live everything. Live the questions now. Perhaps then some
day far in the future, you will gradually, without even noticing it, live
your way into the answer.

Rainer Maria Rilke
(1875-1926)

PART I

Life isn't always what it seems.

The Shower

Acapulco: the last leg of my two week Mexican vacation! How anxious I was for a respite from the singles tour group I traveled with which included thirty women and only one man. Determined just to lull pool-side lapping up exotic drinks from fresh pineapples, I passed up the prepaid boat tour on the second to last day of the trip. I simply couldn't force myself to spend another afternoon bussed around Girl Scout style with a group of giddy women with voracious appetites for worthless trinkets and trivial conversation.

Since my roommate didn't agree with me, she left early in the morning for the tour with the others. For once in the whole trip, I was free to do whatever I wanted without any deadlines for meals or the need to dress up and be sociable. Slipping into my new azure bathing suit, I threw a few things into my beach bag: a cheesy romance novel, sun screen, and a beach towel and then literally skipped to the elevator, singing, "Ah sun and cool water, here I come!"

When I first stretched out at the edge of the pool, I noticed there were very few people around. Among them a handful of young mothers stretched out on lounge chairs keeping tabs on their children playing in the water. They reminded me of some of the women on the tour - flabby, over made up and bored and boring. How happy I was to be rid of all of them for even a short time. I sighed a near swoon of relief, closed my eyes and relaxed. Yoga exercises had really helped me to ease all my tensed muscles completely at will. Oh, how I needed this!

Maybe I dozed for a few minutes or even for a half hour, but when I did open my eyes, I felt exquisitely renewed. There still didn't seem to be anyone around worth getting interested in so I decided it was time to enjoy a fresh Piña Colada. Luxury of luxuries, I simply motioned for one of the roving waiters and gave him my order.

As I sat slowly sipping my luscious tropical pineapple delight, I spied a tall black haired man walking toward me. "If I had to be disturbed by anyone, he would be worth it," I mused, never thinking he would actually stop and talk to me. Surprisingly, though, he did! "The rest of the group could go on their boat tour; I could enjoy a fine diversion right here at the hotel pool," I thought to myself quite happily.

As the two of us kibitzed about the place, the drinks and the water, I realized that not only was Jose good looking, but he also had a remarkably cool and casual yet warm sense of humor. His brown eyes actually seemed to sparkle when he laughed or even smiled. That was what really boiled me over from the beginning. He smiled so easily and laughed so freely. Such a delightful change from the feminine world I had been trapped with for the past ten days.

As we continued our friendly conversation, cliché or not, it did seem like I had known him for a long time so when he asked, "Could you do me a favor? I can't get into my room right now. May I take a shower in yours?" I hesitated a few minutes. My roommate was away on the group tour. What harm would there be to let this guy use our shower?

In my naiveté at the time, I wasn't prepared for the real reason he wanted to come to my room. A roll in the hay at this point in our short acquaintance was simply out of the question.

After I struggled against his advances for what seemed to be a long time, he finally gave up and said he'd take his shower. Relieved, I sat on the bed anxiously waiting for him to finish and be gone. To add insult to injury, he let the water gush out of the shower enclosure and cover the bathroom floor to such a degree that it flowed out into the bedroom. What a mess to clean up.

The next thing I knew he was standing towel-shrouded in front of me. I got up to move over to the window while he dressed. Suddenly, he grabbed my arm and demanded, "That will be two hundred pesos!" Two hundred pesos? What was he talking about? Two hundred pesos for what? For letting him take a shower in my room? I didn't know what to think.

"What are you talking about? Two hundred pesos for what?" The incredulous words stuck to the sides of my mouth.

His nonchalant reply almost knocked me over. "Yes, two

hundred pesos. This is my job. Everyone knows me around here. Two hundred pesos, otherwise there could be trouble."

I caught a glimpse of myself in the dresser mirror at this announcement. My face looked like an avalanche had rolled down on it. His job? What did he do? Who was he? Should I have realized what he was up to? In my state of complete dismay, I couldn't believe I had been so naive to believe his line about needing a shower.

As soon as he got dressed, I somehow managed to push him out the door without giving him even one peso, let alone two hundred. Then I called Sandra, one of my friends who had also decided not to go on the tour that day. She listened to my story and then advised simply, "Just wait for the tour guide when he gets back. He'll know what to do."

Very upset, I went down to the lobby to wait for Mr. Alvarez. I had visions of becoming involved in an international scandal because of my experience with the Two Hundred Peso Man. I wondered if I'd be hassled by the hotel administration or even by an embassy employee for being so naive.

While I sat in the lobby, I noticed Jose on the far side of the area laughing with a group of his friends. I was quite sure I was the brunt of their guffaws.

Finally, Mr. Alvarez came into the hotel. I almost accosted him before he even realized what happened.

"Oh, Mr. Alvarez, I have a big problem...."

"What's the matter, Annie?" he asked looking at me curiously.

"I don't know where to begin. It's all so crazy. I didn't go on the tour today because I just wanted to chill out by the pool. This guy I met asked if he could take a shower in my room. Then...."

"So you let him in and he wanted something else, right?"

"Yes, more... much more than I was willing to give. Oh, I'm such a fool! After I convinced him I wasn't interested, he actually took a shower and then announced that I had to pay him two hundred pesos! I couldn't believe it. He said everyone in the hotel knows what he is and I better pay up or else!" My voice broke at this point, but I forced myself to hold back tears.

"Now settle down, Annie. Stop worrying, this whole deal was one big scam. This guy was certainly not what he implied to you he was. Furthermore, there's nothing he can do to you now." I was so relived as Mr. Alvarez's words penetrated my agitated mind, I almost kissed him on the mouth. He just smiled, though, and left me sitting there in the lobby with tears of relief on my face.

That evening as I sat in the lounge enjoying a Piña Colada with Sandra, Jose came over and knelt down by my chair. "Did you find a key in your room?" he asked.

I assured him I hadn't and told him to get lost.

Hours later, though, when I returned to the "scene of the crime," I noticed his key hanging off the edge of the dresser. I made no attempt to look for him to return it.

Instead I attached it to my house key ring to remind me not to be so awfully naive in the future. It's still there today decades later.

The Drive Through Prague

The two women from London had been waiting impatiently in the lobby of their hotel in old town Prague. Their scheduled vehicle was supposed to arrive to take them to a folklore dance exhibition forty-five minutes ago. Finally, they asked the blond receptionist to call the tour company which booked the transportation.

A cab pulled up outside the entrance fifteen minutes later and Ruth and Cynthia hopped in. Both of them were excited because this exhibition was just what they needed to relax after a rainy day shopping. The driver, whose English was hard to decipher, mentioned what sounded like a street name and asked them if that was where they wanted to go. They assumed the folklore organizers had told him the right destination and admitted they didn't know the address offhand. He responded with "OK" and zipped out into traffic.

After being driven around countless unfamiliar streets and

through endless turns this way and that, they appeared to be no closer to the folklore venue than back at the hotel. The women looked at each other anxiously wondering what they were going to do. The driver didn't speak much English and they didn't speak Czech.

When Cynthia pulled out the flyer for the event and pointed to the address, the man glanced at it and shook his head. She couldn't tell if that meant he understood or not.

Ruth looked at her friend and asked, "What are we going to do? We seem to be driving aimlessly. Are we in trouble, or what?"

"Maybe we're lost. I'll ask him to call the hotel for directions," Cynthia answered. Then she pointed to the name of the hotel and mimicked talking on the phone to the driver. But he just continued to shake his head. Was it yes or no? They couldn't tell.

Minutes later he seemed to talk to the dispatcher on his radio, but unfortunately the women couldn't comprehend a word of the conversation. Hopefully, they were close to the event now. It had started over thirty minutes ago and they really didn't want to miss any more of it.

Both women were trying not to get angry, but they were becoming increasingly nervous as the cab passed through darkened areas across the river outside the city. They realized suddenly that even if they got out, there was no where to go for assistance. There were no gas stations or stores anywhere around. It was 8pm already and every building in sight was dark.

Still the man kept driving. Cynthia and Ruth never were able to enjoy the folklore event....

My Honey Darlin'

"However rare true love may be,
it is less so than true friendship."
La Rochefoucauld

I may be an old lady over ninety years young, but I have what some today would call a Significant Other, a lover by any other name would be as special to me as he is. And he's only in his mid-sixties. His name is Paul, but I call him my Honey Darlin.' OK, go ahead and laugh at me for being so foolish in my advanced age. Just because my skin isn't as smooth as it used to be. Just because I might even have a few little wrinkles here and there. Just because I can't move around very fast anymore. None of that means I don't have some youthful emotions tucked away inside my nine decades body that sometimes show up and surprise me and, if truth be told, maybe a few others as well.

So how did I meet my Honey Darlin'? It was just about five years ago if my memory serves me right. I know it was since I don't have any signs of Alzheimer's. That's for sure.

I was moving in to this apartment right here the same day Paul was moving out of his unit upstairs. What a helpful young man he was to me that day! He carried up box after box for me cutting the time the movers had to work which lowered how much the workers had to be paid. When everything was in, I invited him to stay a bit. I made him coffee and sliced him a big piece of my homemade cinnamon bread. How could I have known that day that every so often he'd drop by in the next weeks and months and now years? Sometimes I called him with a problem I couldn't fix myself like when I wanted to move my sofa to another place in the living room or had to fix the fuse box. He'd take me grocery shopping too and wherever else I had to go like my doctor's or optician's. Other times he'd just come by to visit when he was "in the neighborhood" as he always said. Looking back, I don't know how I survived beforehand without him. All of my children and grandbabies live states away so they can't be here to help me with everyday type things.

My dear Nicky died forty-some years ago. I'm smiling to myself now because I'm thinking that would have been when my Honey Darlin' was hardly thirty and still "wet behind his ears" so to speak. Oh what a great marriage my Nicky and I had enjoying trips with our two daughters and two sons, but like everything else when it was over, it was over and that was that. I never want to be like this woman I know whose husband passed on years ago. One day several years later when I saw her again, I asked if she had ever met anyone else. She just shook her head no and said, "If I even think about it, I imagine Gene up there shaking his finger back and forth." Like he didn't want her to love anyone again? I couldn't accept that. After all, if two people really love each other, they want the other to be happy even when he or she is gone. I know that's what my Nicky would want for me. In fact, he told me that very thing about a month before he died. I remember he said, "Myra, my Love, if you find anyone else, it's fine with me. Grab whatever happiness you can. You deserve it!"

But until I met my Honey Darlin', I never thought I'd even be the least bit interested in another man again. No, it was too hard to imagine feeling all those young emotions again. Still I have to say, it's so very nice, though. Being Paul's special friend has taught me to be open to whatever happens.

So, you might ask, how did I come to call him my Honey Darlin'? Well, one day about a year after I met him when he helped to move me in, he called to ask if I needed to go anywhere. What a nice man even just to check! I told him I'd love it if he would take me shopping. I wanted to buy something new; I just didn't know what. What he couldn't have known was it was my birthday, my ninetieth, so I wanted to buy myself something special to celebrate each of my nine decades on this earth. Paul came and drove me to the local department store.

I went right to the jewelry counter. He followed me but I just shooed him away telling him we didn't have to be joined at the hip while we were there. What I didn't know was that he apparently overheard me telling the salesgirl that I wanted to buy something for my birthday. I didn't say which one though. Probably that cute young salesgirl with three earrings in each lobe thought I had to be at least a hundred anyway. Well, I picked out a lovely silver necklace with a locket on it, a kind I had never owned before in my life. But before I could pay for it, Paul, who forever more I would call my Honey Darlin', stepped beside me and handed the clerk his Visa card. I tried to protest, but he was adamant. Then he took the necklace and put it around my neck saying, "Happy Birthday, Dear One! Come on now, young lady, I'm taking you out for a proper celebration lunch."

Well, what could I say? I must have really overwhelmed the young salesgirl when she saw me looking up into Paul's big blues and heard my reply, "Anything you say, my Honey Darlin'!"

So that's how I fell for this wonderful man and gave him that endearing name. Now some people might wonder if we have any kind of love life. Well, I'm here to say, it's really none of their business. We do, though, I'm happy to admit, but it's not like we're two crazy kids in love. Hardly. We don't do all that touchy feely stuff. Of course, we hug a lot and kiss each other on the cheek, but that is all and enough. I know Paul has to have a life beyond me; I'm not so naive to think otherwise. I am just so happy for whatever time he can spend with me.

One day last week he called me up to ask if he could drop by and bring a friend to meet me. Of course, I agreed. I had no idea at the time to what degree I would be affected by that visit. Several hours later when I answered a knock at my door, I opened it to see my Honey Darlin' standing there beside an attractive brunette about his age or maybe even a few years younger. So she was his friend. Who else should I have expected? He introduced her as a woman he used to work with in another state years before. It was obvious they had a history and maybe more than that together the way they laughed at the same things and looked at each other. Actually, I mean the way he looked at her. I have to admit that green eyed beast named Jealousy was beating down my door the whole time they were here. But what could I do? I stayed as friendly as I could as I smiled, talked and offered them coffee and a piece of my freshly baked cinnamon cake. I almost lost it, as they say, when Paul begged off all of it with, "Thanks, Myra, but Carly and I are off to dinner from here. Some other time." Then before I knew it, my Honey Darlin' and his lovely friend strolled out my door on their way.

Again, I have to admit that this old lady, who hates to even think she's old, still has strong feelings so I cried when they left. I felt so bereft thinking that woman was going to take Paul away from me that I used up almost a whole box of tissues. Then that night I dreamed that my Honey Darlin' and I were in bed together and just as we were about to "get it on" as the young people say today, his friend Carly walked in the room. I woke up shaking all over and crying my eyes out again.

The ringing of the phone startled me and stopped my sobbing. It was Paul. Somehow he had guessed that I might be unhappy after yesterday's visit. He knew me too well. "Myra, how are you doing today? You didn't seem too happy when Carly and I left yesterday."

"Honey Darlin', what makes you say that?"

"Well, I know you well enough to know when you're sad. Please tell me why, Myra."

"I will... but only to please you."

"Well I'm listening. Please tell me."

"Oh, I just had an attack of the blues, feeling sorry for myself, that's all. Nothing for you to get all concerned about, my Honey Darlin.'"

"Wait a minute, Myra. What's this about feeling sorry for yourself? Why?"

"It's just that I'm just an old woman still feeling jealous. Can you believe that?"

"What did you say? Jealous? Of me? Carly?"

"Yes, of both of you."

"But, Myra, Carly and I are just old friends. She was in town yesterday on her way West on a writing grant. I admit at one point or maybe even still to some degree, I would have liked us to be more than friends, but that has never happened."

"Still, Honey Darlin,' she's so pretty and your age and I'm so...."

"Now stop right there, Myra, and hear this. You know and I know age has nothing to do with what you and I have. And hear this further, my friend, Carly is married. Very married, I should say, with a husband who loves her a lot as do her four sons in their twenties, all of whom I've met by the way. Carly and I are good friends, that's all, Myra. Now don't you go on worrying or being jealous or sad about it. I just wanted you two to meet so Carly could see what a fine woman you are, my dear one."

"Oh, my Honey Darlin,' I'm so sorry."

"Now why, Myra?"

"For thinking you were going to throw me over for her. For being so selfish thinking you couldn't have another woman you care about. For being such a foolish old woman."

At that point my Honey Darlin' laughed his inimitable hearty laugh and crooned, "Oh, I do love you, Myra. You are my most special friend and you always will be. Bye now." I almost could feel him kiss my hand when he hung up.

Afterwards I sat staring out the window of my apartment for a long time realizing how fortunate I was to have my Honey Darlin' in my life under whatever circumstances. I may be an old lady and Paul a much younger man, but together knowing what's really on the inside of both of us, we make one fine couple! And no younger woman than I named Carly or whatever else can change that!

Previously published in Ginseng, Summer 2010

The Threat

"**H**ello, are you Jean Marie Tate?"

"Yes...."

"Well, I hear you've been fooling around with my husband. If I ever hear of it again, I'm going to get you, Lady!"

Click. Buzzzzzzzzzzzzzz.

Jean hung up the phone dumbfounded. Who was that woman? She didn't recognize her raspy voice. Who was she talking about? She had been to several singles dances recently but didn't remember giving her number to anyone. In fact, she hadn't even gone out on a date in the past few months let alone "fooled around" with this man as the strange woman on the phone had said.

How did she find out her name and telephone number? Did she search through her husband's jacket and pants' pockets and find a slip of paper with her name and number on it? Had Jean given her number to someone she forgot about? Who could this woman's husband be? Of course, it could have been to some married man she met the last time she went out. How would she have known? After all, some married men did go to singles' dances without wearing their wedding rings. What if this woman is certifiable, who knows what she'd do? Jean had seen more than enough TV shows about women seeking revenge on the lovers of their cheating husbands to know how dangerous they could be even if they acted on erroneous information.

Since she was scheduled to be at the home of a student she was tutoring in the next hour, Jean knew she had to get moving to get there on time or a few minutes early as usual. As she walked to her car, she looked around the parking lot of her apartment complex. "Could the woman from the phone be waiting for me out here? Would she follow me wherever I go?" Jean didn't have a clue but decided she'd better not take any chances. She'd be on the lookout for her just in case.

As a result, all the way to Derrick's home she kept an eagle eye on her rear view mirror searching for any sign of a car following her. Ten minutes into her drive she saw a black Cadillac swerve across a lane and pull up right behind her. But when she looked closer, she realized the driver was a middle-aged man apparently wearing a chauffeur's hat. As he passed her, she noted the name of a rental company on the side of the car but didn't see anyone sitting in the back seat. She figured the driver was just in a hurry to pick up his next customer.

To calm herself, Jean flipped on her favorite 50's station and started to sing along with what she considered to be the Coasters' best song, "In the Still of the Night." Suddenly without warning, a red Ford pushed into her back fender, hitting it ever so carefully it seemed to her.

And there was a woman at the wheel!

Now Jean was really concerned. Could she be the woman who threatened her on the phone earlier? Why would she now be trying to mess up her car in this way? Or was she just some weird woman losing control of her car?

"No, this was too orchestrated," Jean said out loud to herself. "Now what should I do? Is there a police station nearby?" But she didn't know the immediate area well enough to find one. The dangerous woman was still on her tail. How long could she keep this up? She hoped her student's home was only a minute or two away. As soon as she saw the street, she took a quick right onto it. To her relief the red Ford kept going! Maybe it was another threat if, in fact, the driver was the same woman who threatened her on the phone.

While she was at her student's home, she became completely focused on the work as she routinely did so the tutoring hour passed quickly. She enjoyed helping Derrick practice SAT related work - vocabulary study, subject/verb agreement, sentence structure and, of course, writing.

Afterwards to her chagrin as she walked out to her car in the driveway, she noticed a red Ford three driveways down. "Could it have be the same one that had followed me?" she asked herself. "If so, did the woman who had threatened me live there?" She left with more unanswered questions than she had an hour earlier.

On her way home she became more paranoid, carefully watching every car that pulled anywhere near hers especially ones with women at the wheel. It seemed to her that red Fords kept multiplying on the road. Was it just her imagination or were there actually an increasing number of them all around her?

By the time she walked into her apartment, still nervous from the strain of her trip home, Jean was shaking all over and perspiring through her shirt. When she noticed the light flashing on her answering machine, she was afraid to hit the button for the message.

When she reluctantly did, all she heard was hysterical laughing and then a resounding, "I got you!" It was her crazy friend Amy's voice. Jean remembered her older sister was home from college and that she drove a red Ford.

Gene flicked off the machine still oddly unnerved.

The Way They Began

Early one morning recently a distraught woman walking aimlessly across the beach at Nag's Head, North Carolina. Depressed. Distracted.

A guy with his dog running at the edge of the water. Frolicking. Laughing. Having fun in the early sun of the day.

Suddenly the woman running right into the man's arms. So overwhelmed by her sadness, not seeing the man and dog in her path....

The shock of remembrance. He, a pragmatic romantic, recalls her as "The Brain" from high school, always aloof in her own world of study, study, study. Not "with it" like the popular girls he went out with then. The man now ensconced in his marketing career. Happy with just himself and his Golden Retriever Henry and a New York State of Mind. Open. Expansive. Adventurous.

She, a controlled romantic and an inveterate Barbra Streisand fan, only recalls him as a jerk from those days, someone she wouldn't even look at, let alone even consider talking to then.

She is locked in a small town closed state of mind. Extremely religious. Uptight. Very serious. She can only buy "on sale" clothes. She is rather depressed because her life has not been going the way she had hoped, stuck for the past five years in a unpleasant job with no future and especially no fun.

No romance in her life either. Her Catholic brainwashing had left her single with no possibility of "getting lucky" so she remained alone and sad. Alone since a forced-on-her-part platonic affair with one of her professors at graduate school, a man with a wife her age and two toddlers. Every time she thinks about him, she hears Streisand sing, "You used to hate to leave me... but used to be's don't count anymore; they just lay on the floor until we sweep them away... I learned how to love and how to lie. You think I could learn how to tell you good bye."

If the man the woman ran into had known in advance what the woman's main hangup was, would he have been able to deal with her reticence for sexual involvement? Her strong belief about no sex until marriage? He wasn't interested in that route. Very happy with Henry for a friend, he had women only "on the side" when he needed release. After all, a dog doesn't talk back, criticize, or bamboozle him to clean up on weekends when he flips from being a well-dressed businessman and regresses to the playboy status of his younger days.

The woman is hung up on her former "lover." Scarred and stunned by the end of her relationship, platonic as it was, with her professor, she lives Barbra's lyrics as a theme song for their doomed relationship. "Coming in and out of your life isn't easy when they're are so many nights I can't hold you... I don't need to touch you to feel you. It's so real with you. I can't get you out of my mind but I can remember."

Because of her religious conditioning, she's still a virgin at thirty though in her heart she was her professor's lover. "Her" Tom was married and with children he would not and could not leave for her. How was she to face the dead end of their relationship and get beyond it so it wasn't so paramount to her? "Coming in and out of your life isn't easy. I don't need to touch you to feel you." She had sent him a CD of this song, but he never acknowledged getting it. She wondered if he ever even listened to it or understood what she was telling him with its lyrics.

And now what had she done? Inadvertently running into this jerk she hardly knew in high school who's a grown man now so virile and handsome with sparkling deep blue eyes and lots of black curly hair accentuating his six foot muscled body. A cute dimple on his chin too and the beginning of a three o'clock shadow even in this early hour. And, most of all, an engaging smile which sent shivers throughout her body on this warm morning stirring something inside her as though he had flipped a switch on in her body, lighting up the darkest places of her unhappy self. And his dog seemed to take to her almost instantly, jumping up and licking her face. She had the uncanny sense he was trying to tell her something important, but he stopped abruptly at his owner's command, "OK, Henry, that's enough!"

What the woman didn't know was that the guy had been a macho guy in his teens as a cover for his inveterate insecurity and lack of self esteem. Even though he had a real knack of getting it on with easy girls. Burned a number of times by ones he somewhat cared about who dropped him with no explanation, he continued searching for what some women would call "The One."

Did those who rejected him see through his macho facade or did they always want more than he was willing to give? He never knew; he just refused even to try to understand them then. In his twenties, though, he enjoyed several more serious connections, but he still kept his mask on. As a result no one could really see behind it to find out who he really was. He never gave any of the women he dated a chance to get to know the real man inside the closed room of himself.

But for the few fleeing seconds this beach walker woman was in his arms, he unwittingly felt something shift inside his well-toned body as though the mortar between the bricks of his personality facade was loosening. It was as though the woman waved a wand with her body making him fall for her instead of her literally falling into his arms.

When she ran into him out of the blue, all his senses went on high alert. He smelled her coconut sun screen and felt its moisture that remained on her skin. Her apology, "I'm so sorry. I wasn't paying any attention," seemed to float up out of the warm sand. He tasted salt on his lips as he responded, "No problem." Then he was shaken by the full sight of her in a one piece black suit which covered her shapely body quite attractively. Her light brown short hair glowed in the sunlight, her green-brown eyes twinkled. "Not exactly an Awesome Ten but definitely an Extremely Enchanting Eight!" he thought to himself.

For several minutes the man and the woman stood inches apart staring into each other's eyes as though they had been transported to some other reality beyond this world. How could they have known then that both of their futures would be irrevocably bound together from that first short encounter?

As the woman pulled away from the man, she murmured, "Sorry" again and continued her aimless walk down the beach. The man stood watching her for a long time until his breathing stabilized and he felt his dog jumping up and down on him. "OK, Henry. We'll run some more now. What do I care about some crazy woman who can't even see us right in front of her? You and me, that's all I need, right, old boy?"

For herself the woman couldn't get the handsome man and his Golden Retriever out of her mind even when she finally stopped walking and sank down on the warm sand under an umbrella someone had left on the beach. She let the in-and-out flow of the waves mesmerize her for a few moments.

When her eyes closed, she only saw "her" Tom. Oh how she loved that man despite his other life and commitments! His creative searching mind. His loving warm body against hers when he held her in his arms, the only physical contact with him she'd allow because of her strict religious upbringing. Everything about him had stirred her to want more of him. The more of him he could never have given her even if she could have ever agreed to the taking. Again words from one of Barbra's songs ran through her mind. "Memories like the color of my mind... misty water colored memories of the way we were.... Can it be it was all so simple then? If we had the chance to do it all again, tell me would we, could we?"

And now here she was alone. Bereft without him. Sad and depressed. Still wanting "her" Tom more than she could admit to herself. But yet knowing she could never really have him, the faint hope she'd been hanging onto all but dissipated. She realized finally with a shock to her whole system that whatever they had had together was over. Done. Finished. Ended. She couldn't let herself be with him ever again. He had a life she could never share. But now she had no one to talk to. No one to share her deepest yearnings with. No one to share her dreams and joys or tell her worries to. "Ohhh!" she sighed distraught.

"So why the big sigh?" she heard a deep voice ask bringing her out of her reverie. For a wonderful second she almost believed it was "her" Tom, but then she opened her eyes and saw the smiling face of the man she had run into earlier instead.

"As I said, why the big sigh?" he asked again.

Managing a slight smile, she replied, "Just remembering someone."

"Well, why don't you get up and walk with us to get your mind off whoever's making you look so sad?"

"Oh no, I couldn't do that. I know we went to the same high school, but I have to admit I don't remember your name."

"I'm Pete. Pete Johnson. And my hound here is Henry. And I think I remember you're Marcie, Marcie McDane, right?"

"No, it's McLane. Thank you again for catching me earlier, Pete." At that she reached out and hugged his Golden Retriever. His owner smiled his engaging smile and grabbed Marcie's hand, "Come on, join us on our walk."

If any beach watchers had noticed the man and the woman and the dog as they made their way across the edge of the water then, they might have thought they were just an ordinary couple walking their pet on the beach. They could never have imagined all the baggage they were also carrying with them that they'd have to sort out apart and together as time went by.

As for themselves, Marcie and Pete would never have been able to admit to each other this fine morning, that this new couple, because couple they were already, had fallen in love at first sight or actually at first touch. Their lives had been forever changed from their first moment of contact.

No more walking alone or just with a dog down the Beach of Life. Their futures were now intertwined "from this day forward, for better, for worse, for richer, for poorer, in sickness and in health...."

Lila, The Love of His Lonely Life

For thirty of his fifty years Henry Arnold was known as Brother Charles, a monk in a contemplative order. Though the community kept a Vow of Silence except for conferences with the Abbot, confessions and an occasional recreation hour with their fellow monks, they remained out of touch with the world at large. Last month Brother Charles was assigned a unique job by his superior - to watch the nightly news and then report the major events from around the country and the world on the bulletin board so that all the brothers would have specific intentions for their prayers.

There was only one problem with Brother Charles' new job. Inexplicably, it led him to fall in love with the Evening Newscaster, a woman in her thirties with flowing shoulder length blond hair, a sweet engaging smile and, as far as he was concerned, perfect bronzed features. She looked like his Mother Lila and her Mother Lily when they were the same age though their hair was put up in different styles then. The old family photos hardly did them justice. In his mind he called the TV woman Lila after his Mother.

Most of all, though, the woman on the news reminded him of his high school girlfriend Sylvia whom he had found out through Lila had been killed recently in a head on collision on a local freeway. He had intended to marry her after they both got their BA's, but like Steinbeck's "best laid plans of mice and men," things just didn't work out that way between them. Sylvia was determined to go to med school across country after college delaying any possibility of an ongoing relationship and certainly marriage and a family for at least a decade or more. He couldn't wait. He told himself it was because he couldn't live without her, but that wasn't the real reason....

Distracted momentarily from his job with these thoughts, Brother Charles brought his attention back to the TV and to Lila, the Love of His Lonely Life. She was doing a news story now on a terrorist attack in a town in India that used to be called Bombay. He watched appalled by the first reports of many dead and wounded including Americans as well as the massive destruction of two hotels and a train station. By the time the ads came on, he felt like he was going to throw up, but when his lovely Lila reappeared on the screen all his upset evaporated into the stale air of the small room where he sat enamored of her. As he gazed into her eyes, he imagined she was reporting the news solely for him. What a unique "tête-à-tête" they had then!

Brother's ongoing problem was he couldn't get Lila, the Love of His Lonely Life, out of his mind, not that he really wanted to. She smiled at him through his daily prayers from Vigils before dawn though Vespers at dusk. Even during Mass. It was like she was praying with him throughout the day. After a few weeks of watching her on the evening news, Brother Charles started to feel that she was actually in the room with him. He knew on some level of his logical self that she was just an image on the flashing screen of the monk's lone fifteen inch TV, but in his emotional self she was as real to him as any of the brothers he broke bread with three times a day and prayed and worked with together at other times.

One evening as he sat engrossed listening to Lila, the Love of His Lonely Life, discuss the problems of the Stock Market and the retailers in the area, he was startled and jumped up suddenly when his Abbot touched him on his shoulder and directed, "Brother Charles, please turn off the TV. I have some sad personal news for you."

The monk reluctantly did as he was told and stood up to hear what his superior had to tell him. "Brother, it's Regina. She's had a massive heart attack."

"Is she OK?"

"No, I'm sorry to say. She isn't. Since you're her only sibling, you may take the morning train to be with her family. She has several teenage sons, doesn't she? "

"Yes, she does. I'm really worried about them. Their father was killed in Iraq five years ago. My sister has been raising the boys by herself since then. What will happen to them? I'm the only member of their immediate family left."

"Don't worry about that now, Brother. Just go and give them all the support you can and make the arrangements for them."

"Thank you, Father, but what about my news reporting?"

"I've asked Brother Simon to take over. Now go in as much

peace as you can, Brother. You will find the answers you need with God's help."

That night Henry aka Brother Charles didn't sleep well at all. He kept wondering if Brother Simon would fall in love with his Lila too. Nightmares stormed through his mind every time he closed his eyes. First, his sister Regina was smiling at him. Then she became Lila, the Love of His Lonely Life, and in turn his Mother and Grandmother. All of them dissolving one by one into a caldron of raging fire. Oddly, he woke up shivering.

When he finally pulled himself out of bed to get ready to leave the monastery, he was in no shape to drive to the train station. Fortunately, one of the maintenance workers took the wheel of the community's beat up Ford ready to do the honors. It seemed to him that every blond woman he saw on the train was Lila, the Love of His Lonely Life. When he went to the club car for lunch, he was overjoyed to actually see her on a flat screen TV reporting the noon news and in a sense eating with him too. He stayed in the car drinking cup after cup of coffee until she signed off and he was shooed out by the waiters so they could clean up after the lunch crowd.

An hour later, the train stopped at the station before his destination. To his absolute dismay Lila, the Love of His Lonely Life, sat down in the empty seat beside him! He knew he had now lost all touch with reality. There was no way she could be on this train with him. She had the news to do. She lived in the TV, didn't she? How could she now have a flesh and blood body to sit down beside him? Oh, he knew he was losing it...

When he woke up from his afternoon nap, he almost cried out,

"Lila, where are you?" since no one was sitting beside him. No beautiful woman. And certainly no Lila, the Love of His Lonely Life. He looked at his watch. He'd arrive at his stop in fifteen minutes. How had he slept so long?

He thought he caught a glimpse of Lila again as he waited for his nephew who had just gotten his driver's license to pick him up, but it was a false alarm. Only some dyed blond who looked like a frown was drawn indelibly on her face. He sighed as he climbed into Liam's car and was driven to the family's home in the suburbs.

All the arrangements, the funeral and the luncheon afterwards passed in a whiteout of a snow storm as far as Brother Charles was concerned. If someone had asked him the next evening everything that had happened, he wouldn't have been able to say. He had loved Regina deeply as only a big brother could. With her gone he felt bereft and, what's more, extremely concerned about the welfare of his nephews - Hank fourteen and the little guy Timmy ten. There was no way in God's good earth that they were going into foster care, he resolved. He had to step up to the plate and be their new Mom and Dad combined. He was sure the Abbot would give him a Leave of Absence for the time being. Then eventually he'd have to decide whether to leave the community for good or find some other way for the boys to be taken care of. But definitely not, though, by foster parents. He had heard entirely too many horror stories about how some of those folks mistreated their wards. He vowed his nephews would never be stuck in that system of possible or probable abuse with all the repercussions into the future for them.

As he presumed, his Abbot was more than understanding about

his predicament. He willingly agreed to give him a Leave of Absence with Brother's promise that he'd make a decision about staying or leaving the community within the next six months. Brother Charles agreed, returned to the monastery for his few possessions and found himself back on the train to his sister's house within a few days after her funeral.

This time he knew for sure that Lila, the Love of His Lonely Life, sat down beside him. Her voice was the same as on the TV when she asked him softly, "Is this seat taken?" Her hair, her face, her whole self was there, not just her TV persona. He actually felt her soft arm brush against his as she sat down. He felt completely conflicted and confused. Why was she on this train? Didn't she have the news to prepare and then deliver? Brother Simon would be ready with pen and paper at the monastery. What was happening?

He squeaked out a response, "No, please sit down. I'm Bro...I mean Henry. And you are...?"

"Well, hi, Henry. I'm Sarah Sondheim. You may have seen me on the Channel 4 news."

"Oh, yes, that's where I saw you, Lila... I mean Sarah. You see, I watch the evening news so I can report what's happening in the world to my brothers at the monastery. So why are you on this train today? Don't you have to be at the station preparing for tonight's program?"

"No, Henry, I have the day off. You see I just found out an old girlfriend Regina from one of my college classes recently died. I'm going to Chester to see the family since I missed her funeral."

"Wait a minute. You wouldn't be referring to Regina Westwood, could you?"

"How did you know that, Henry? Wait a minute! Are you her older brother she used to talk about all the time? I thought she told me you went to a monastery many years ago."

"I did but you probably don't know that Regina's husband was killed in Iraq five years ago so now after my sister's death, their two sons, the youngest only ten, are orphans. I'm their only family so...."

"Oh I'm so sorry Jim's gone too. So you've left the order then?"

"Not exactly. I mean not completely until I can decide what's best for my nephews."

"Well, that means you have some big decisions to make, don't you?"

The conductor collecting tickets had to call out to him loudly as though shaking him back to reality in this voice, "May I have your ticket, Sir?"

Henry looked up at the man discombobulated and confused and asked, "Where's Lila? Did she leave me again? Oh, what's happening to me?"

The conductor just shook his head and kept walking.

By the time Henry connected with Liam again with his two brothers in tow, he wasn't sure what was real or not. His nephews couldn't reach him though they tried with lots of crazy talk about school and music and the latest popular movies.

Henry just stared out the window wondering, "Where has my Lila, the Love of My Lonely Life, gone?" He had no idea.

The Couple at the Café

I watched him walking back and forth outside the window of the café in Vienna, Austria where my friend Frank and I sat enjoying an early dinner of Wiener Schnitzel. A rather handsome man wearing a grey suit, he held a mobile phone in his ear as he paced to and fro gesticulating.

I was curious about his conversation, who he was talking to, and whether it was for business or pleasure. Minutes later, he walked into the restaurant and sat half on the stool of the bar with one leg on the floor, obviously waiting for someone.

Surprisingly, he continued to talk on his cellular phone even when a casually dressed black haired woman came in and sat down on the stool next to him. Intermittently for the next fifteen minutes, we noticed that as he talked, he would occasionally kiss the woman on the cheek or she'd put her head on his shoulder. Then at one point they sat kissing on the lips for several moments.

I couldn't help but wonder what the person on the phone was saying while this man and woman openly showed their affection for each other. Was his wife complaining about something their children did or an appliance on the blink or a new bill they hadn't planned for? Or was he listening to problems one of his children had at school while he sipped his red wine and made out with the woman? Or was it a business associate talking about a big deal in the offering, big enough that he stayed on the phone despite his woman friend's presence?

Frank and I left the café never knowing what became of the man on the cell phone and the woman patiently waiting by his side in the Viennese restaurant on that autumn night. Later, as we walked down the street past other restaurants filled with people with their own stories, I couldn't stop thinking about the couple at the café so I convinced Frank to go back there with me. When we returned to the establishment, they were still there. The show must go on as they say.

We sat down and drank Wieselburger beer as I kept watching the infamous couple at the bar. As the man continued to talk on his little phone for what was now at least twenty minutes, suddenly the woman with him hopped off her stool, knocking her glass of wine all over him. Then she stormed out of the restaurant. I couldn't believe it; the man just brushed off his pants and continued talking.

After paying our tab, Frank and I walked out the front door where two men were blabbering on their respective mobile phones. Were they being impolite as well? Who was waiting patiently for them? Wife, mistress, children? I decided I couldn't be bothered by any of this another minute as we waved down the first cab.

Masquerades

"We all wear masks on occasion even the good
but especially the dishonorable." Anon.

S he'd been feeling depressed for so long she didn't know when it started or what precipitated it. She tried to go on with her life as best she could following her normal routine to the letter so no one else would know the depths to which she had sunk. When she smiled, it was like she was on stage in a drama pretending to be a happy carefree young woman. Her Mother had always said she was a wonderful actress, but she knew she was now playing the biggest role of her life pretending everything was all right.

Unconsciously, she knew she was not meant for her current life of penance and deprivation as a nun, but she couldn't confront this awareness directly. As a result she couldn't put her finger on the cause of her pain and went through the motions required by the way of life she had chosen after graduating from high school. She wanted to be a good nun but could only hardly maintain the facade of being one. She didn't know how long she'd be able to keep it up.

One night despite her firm resolve to keep her depression secret, she tossed and turned in her single white sheeted bed without respite. Both surcease of her depression into the oblivion of dreams and relaxation of her disturbed body eluded her. Frustrated, she dragged herself out of bed and began walking up and down the hall of the building where she had been assigned to live with her fellow young nuns attending college. She paced all night with no relief from the gloom surging through her soul.

Of course, she was sure now that one of the other good nuns would inform her superior so she wasn't the least surprised when she returned to her room just after daybreak to find a folded sheet of paper under her door with the handwritten words, "Mother Evelyn would like to see you at 11 o'clock" on it. Since it was Saturday, she didn't have any college classes so she walked across the driveway to her superior's first floor office and knelt down by her desk as was the custom.

"I'll get right to the point, Sister. I understand you haven't been feeling like yourself lately even pacing the hall all last night. Please tell me what's bothering you. I want to help you in whatever way I can."

Sister Martha couldn't look up into her superior's eyes. She felt so weak and ungrateful feeling so depressed. After all, the community took care of all her physical needs so well - food, shelter, clothes, books and whatever other necessities. Still it wasn't and hadn't been enough for her for some time. She really wanted to explain all of this to Mother Evelyn, but the words wouldn't form into sentences she could say out loud. All she could do was stammer a partial answer. "I.... I don't feel... well or... I mean... I feel down... I..."

"But, Sister, you always appear so happy. All the sisters like you. You're following the Rule exactly. You're making excellent grades in all your courses. I don't understand what's the matter. Please tell me."

Sister Martha replied in one breath to get it out as quickly as possible, "Oh, Mother Evelyn, I'vebeensodepressedforalongtime I'magoodactresslikemyMotheralwaystold me."

"But, why didn't you tell me about this problem before now, Sister Martha?"

On the verge of tears, the young nun replied, "Oh, Mother, I was embarrassed and so scared thinking you'd send me home for not being a good sister."

"But, Sister Martha, that's not how we do things here. We all help each other and care about each other's needs and concerns. Especially me."

Mother Evelyn recalled how many times she struggled with depression especially during her early days in the community more than thirty years ago, but she always managed to get beyond those down feelings by becoming an inveterate workaholic immersing herself in constant activities to blanket over the pain. She would have died if it hadn't been for her friendship with Zack. There was no way she'd let depression ruin this poor young nun. No, she'd take action right away to see that she got the help she needed.

"Sister, I'm going to arrange for you to talk to Father Zachary. I feel confident he will be able to help you pull yourself out of your depression. He's the pastor at Saint John's in town. We studied psychology together at Stanford. I'll give you money for transportation to his rectory and arrange a companion to go with you."

"Oh, but, Mother, I.... I... I would rather not.... tell a stranger my problems.... I..."

"But I insist, Sister. You need to do this for your own good. God be with you."

From her office window Mother Evelyn watched Sister Martha walk slowly back to her building, but all her thoughts centered on Zack. She didn't think anyone knew she had fallen in love with him when she was just about Sister Martha's age. Or that over the past three decades he had frequently urged her to go to bed with him, but she remained true to her vow of Chastity and rejected his advances. She refused to believe the rumors about his questionable behavior she'd overheard some of the nuns whisper recently. There was no way he could be anything but good. She really believed he was the one to help Sister Martha just like the other new nuns she had sent to see him over the years.

Several days later Sister Martha and her friend Sister Mary Arthur rode the local bus to Saint John's. On the way they talked quietly.

"Mary Arthur, I really don't want to be doing this."

"I know you don't, but hopefully it's for the best. To get you some long overdue relief."

"That's what Mother Evelyn says. Still I'm doing this under duress."

When the two nuns arrived at the rectory, the priest's elderly housekeeper wearing a long dark dress with an equally long starched white apron tied over it ushered Sister Martha into a room down the hall from the one where she told her companion to wait. As she sat nervously in a comfortable chair, Sister looked around the sparsely decorated room. Only a crucifix hung on one of the walls. On the far side of the room stood a cluttered desk with a chair behind it. Another chair waited empty across from the one where she sat. In her agitated state it seemed like hours before a tall middle aged priest sauntered into the room. He smiled at the nun, called her by name and announced his in a flourish. Then he peered at her and asked, "How can I help you, Sister?"

Sister Martha could not lift her eyes to look into his. Instead, she stared at the floor where the priest's spit polished black shoes tapped on the maroon carpet. At a loss for words, she could only stammer, "I... that is, Mother Evelyn sent me. She said you could... get me... I mean... help me... get out of... my.... "

"...depression," the priest filled in. "Yes, Mother Evelyn told me that you haven't been feeling well." He stared at the young nun sitting across from him who could feel his eyes looking almost through her. He noticed that her hands were extremely white and looked very delicate. Her nails short. Her floor length habit neatly kept. No stains apparent on it or on her rounded front piece he knew the nuns called a guimpe. With her eyes looking down at the floor, he couldn't tell their color or see the youthful skin on her face, but he had noted both when she glanced up at him when he first came into the room. Her eyes were light brown and her face without blemish. She was a beauty! He felt his loins struggling with this realization. In his weakness despite years of therapy, he knew he could easily give in to this temptation especially since he had recently returned to the bottle to assuage his pain. Celibacy has been a thorn in his side since the day he was ordained a priest three decades ago. Suddenly, he felt himself become quite warm and asked the young nun, "Do you mind if I open the window a few inches, Sister?"

"No, Father."

When the priest sat down again, he continued to peer at the young nun sitting in front of him. There was no question in his mind that she was extremely depressed floundering in a pit of darkness. He knew the signs. In fact, he had lived them all himself. A total dissatisfaction with everything and everyone especially himself. A gnawing pain like a heavy steel door closing on top of him. A deep feeling of worthlessness and despair. It had started so many years ago he couldn't remember exactly when any more than Sister could pinpoint the beginning of her depression. Before it all started, he had been so intent on having Evelyn's love, but she rejected his bodily expression of it. Every time he took another young nun into his care, it was only Evelyn he saw. Only her as the very young nun he met at graduate school. In the past few years he had found a way to assuage some of the pain he constantly suffered by his special way to pull others out of their own.

He forced himself to end his reverie and tried to get Sister to tell him how she felt. To open up to him so he could help her. Again he felt very warm thinking about her opening up to him. Such a lovely young woman. Almost certainly a virgin. When would she have had any chances at love having entered the community at only sixteen as

Evelyn had told him? He made himself look out the window at the now falling rain for a distraction as he waited for the nun to answer his next question, "So, Sister, why don't you tell me when you first started to feel depressed?"

Sister Martha barely glanced up at the man in black and stammered, "I don't really know... maybe.... some time last month... no... last year.... I've been feeling so bad for so long... I just don't remember... exactly when it... started."

"But do you recall what made you begin to feel this way, Sister? Did anything in particular happen?"

"No.... I can't put my finger... on anything.... unless...."

Again, as Father waited for the young nun to continue, he had the sense that just taking her so white and delicate hands in his would help her to go on. Yes, that's what he would do to begin to help her. At the priest's first touch Sister Martha recoiled immediately as though a sizzling hot iron had branded her hand, but when she realized his hand felt so cool and reassuring, she let down her guard and didn't pull hers away from his. For several long minutes the two sat quietly hand in hand as Zack felt himself getting warmer and warmer. Then from somewhere deep in his groin he heard a seething warning, "Slow down, you old fool, or else!"

Sister Martha, on the other hand, was feeling calmer and calmer. She was relaxing now feeling the priest's strength flow into her body. It had been a long time since she felt so good.

Then suddenly sirens blared in her head, "No contact. Move away!" As she did, she almost knocked the priest off his chair and could only stammer an apology, "Oh, I'm... so sorry... Father. I.... I..."

as she glanced for a split second into the man's hooded deep blue eyes.

Startled and disconcerted as though the young nun's innocent gaze had penetrated to the depths of his troubled soul, Father Zachary got up and walked over to the window again lifting it half way up this time. When he returned to his seat, Sister Martha's head was down once more. He had to try a different tack to release the pain she'd obviously been enduring for a long time.

Sister Martha was mortified at her actions. Letting the priest hold her hand. Looking up into his eyes. Almost knocking him out of his seat when she suddenly pulled her hand away from his. She didn't know what to say or do next. Actually, now she was feeling worse than she did before she first met this man. For some reason she couldn't comprehend he had began to scare her. Though now feeling extremely uneasy in his presence, she knew she couldn't leave. She had promised Mother Evelyn. She'd just have to deal with her fear somehow.

Then she heard the priest asking her, "Sister Martha, aren't you going to make your First Profession soon?"

"Yes, Father. In six months."

"How old will you be then?"

"Nineteen. I entered at sixteen because I graduated from high school ahead of time since I skipped two grades in elementary school. Everyone said I was too young to give my life to God, but I knew in my heart it was meant to be so I left my parents, two brothers and three sisters and my high school boyfriend and all my other friends and everything I loved to do like dance, buy nice clothes, go to the beach. I follow the Rule so well now I even feel guilty for those who don't, but it's no good. I feel terrible. I'm so unhappy and depressed all the time."

Father was taken aback. This was the most Sister had said since he sat down with her. What else must be vying for attention inside her? How much more had she refused to deal with and tried to ignore? She had become a huge infected sore that had festered out of control due to lack of attention, medication and loving understanding.

Then against his better judgment and all his education and position and even common sense, he announced as sincerely as he could, "Oh, dear Sister Martha, I have one way proven to make you feel better. Much better. Follow me please."

Like a robot Sister Martha pulled herself up from her chair and walked behind the priest. Something told her she should turn around instead and hurry back to the room where Sister Mary Arthur was waiting for her, but her feet wouldn't cooperate with that thought. Instead she followed the priest out a side door she hadn't even noticed was in the room until he opened it. Overwhelmed, she realized he was leading her into his bedroom! Her life, her body and soul, her conscience and her future were to be forever changed in the next ten minutes....

$\sim$ ∞

"Oh my sweet girl, why did this have to happen to you? Why that priest should have his balls cut off! Imagine trying to make you feel better by making him feel fine! I can't believe it!"

"Still and all you can't tell anyone, Ted. Please promise me."

Cindy, the former Sister Martha, was sitting now in the living room of her parents' home talking to her high school boyfriend. After a few glasses of red wine, she relaxed and let her story flow out to him. Why she left the convent. Why she felt even more depressed now months later. And why she now wanted some way to get back at her former superior and her friend, the "good" Father. Ted was the only one she had told what really happened that fateful day she went to see the priest who promised to make her feel better and had subsequently ruined her life.

"Well, do you promise me or not, Ted?" she asked her friend again.

"Of course, I do, Cindy. You knew I would. Otherwise you wouldn't have told me the disgusting details of what led you to leave the convent and make you want to get back at that superior who sent you to that horrible waste of skin of a priest. So what are we going to do about them?"

"Wait a minute. What do you mean 'we' are going to do? This is my problem, Ted."

"But, Cindy, you know how much I've always cared about you even after you entered the convent and nearly broke my heart. I have to help you get back at these disgusting people."

Ted had been in love with Cindy from when they first met as teenagers. When she told him she was going to enter the convent, he grieved for her as though she had just told him she had a terminal illness and was about to die. Still he wanted her to be happy and do what she had to do, leaving him wounded and in great pain. Certainly, he was ecstatic then when she left but devastated when she told him why.

"Oh, Ted, it's just so hard trying to come up with a way to retaliate. Maybe I should just drop the whole thing. It's not a very nice idea after all. Revenge."

"No way! We'll think of something."

"Or you will, right?"

"You know I will. I have to take off to work now. My mind is in hypermode, though, thinking of a Plan with a capital P. I'll call you later. Bye, Cindy."

After Ted left for work, Cindy curled up on the sofa and fell into a disturbed sleep....

Again and again she felt herself being forced open. Open in an area where she had never even touched herself. On a blood covered bed a hairy old man on top of her relentlessly insisting, "Relax now, Sister!" In horror she screamed as though she was being murdered....

"Wake up, Honey. Did you have another one of your nightmares, dear?" Her Mother was sitting next to her talking to her in her usual soothing voice.

Restraining a sob, Cindy answered, "Yes, Mom." Then a cascade of tears flowed down her face.

"You've had a lot of those lately, Honey. Do they have anything to do with your leaving the convent? Please talk to me. I want you to be your happy self again."

"Oh, Mom, don't worry. I just haven't figured out what to do with the rest of my life yet, but I'll work things out."

These words made some sense to Mrs. Arnold so she slowly got up from the sofa and softly said to her daughter, "OK, Honey, if that's how you want it. Dinner will be ready in an hour. I'm making your favorite - roast vegetables with wild rice and blackberry pie à la mode for dessert. You call me if you need anything."

Cindy frowned as her Mother left the room. She hoped against hope that Ted would come up with an idea soon that would help rid her of the pain. She wanted to will Old Man Depression, who had become her constant companion, to be gone, but she didn't have much energy left to fight "him" off any longer. She considered herself a completely worthless person who permitted an even more worthless person to con her into giving up her virginity supposedly to make herself feel better. When in actual fact it only made him feel good and destroyed her and her vocation. Now she felt she was sitting on a precipice dangling her feet over the edge all but ready to let herself fall into the total darkness below.

That night when she woke shaking uncontrollably and perspiring profusely through her nightgown after yet another reliving of that afternoon in Father Zachary's bed, she stumbled into the bathroom. In a daze she swallowed several handfuls of her antidepressant pills. In the early morning her Mother found her lifeless body sprawled out on her bedroom floor.

When Ted heard the news, he was completely devastated and extremely angry. Now more than ever he had to find a way to get revenge on that man and woman, those purported Holy Ones of God! And to think one was the Mother Superior on a community and the other one a priest on the fast track to becoming a Monsignor! "Isn't there anyone in this world who can be trusted?" he wondered.

At the funeral home he looked lovingly at his friend's beautiful shell of a body for the last time and promised, "I will find a way, Cindy, very soon. You can count all the stars in Heaven on that, my Love!"

The answer to his search for a Plan came to him in a snippet of a dream the next night....

He sat looking at a photo of his friend Cindy when she was Sister Martha, but instead he saw his face not hers!

The next morning the dream answer became absolutely clear to him. He would pursue his vendetta against the community by hurting them from the inside. He would cross dress as a woman and enter Sister Martha's community to get a number of the new nuns to leave. He asked his close doctor friend to cover for him as a "her." Dr. Sam agreed because he knew the trauma Sister Martha suffered after her rape having been the physician she had seen under false pretenses to Mother Evelyn at the time. Ted's Plan was not to hurt anyone like the "good" priest had done but simply to turn each of the young nuns on so they would want to leave the community and not take their vows, especially the one called Chastity. This wholesale leave taking would make Mother Evelyn and also Father Zachary be considered failures for not being able to help the young nuns and hopefully lead the Powers that Be above them to remove them from their positions of authority.

With his curly blond hair and genetic face condition that forestalled his having to shave as well as his short stature of 5'5", Ted wearing a specially designed brunette wig entered the community without any problems and became "Sister Alberta." A Sister Teresa, only a year older, became his Angel or the special person to show "her" the ropes in the beginning.

Unfortunately for Ted, before he could make any significant inroads on the young nuns, he was found out without warning one morning in the communal bathroom. In a major hurry because he had waited too long to leave a spiritual direction class, he lunged into the first of the six stalls forgetting to lock the door. When Sister Teresa also hurried into the room some minutes later and threw open the same door, to her dismay she saw him as "Sister Alberta" sitting on the commode with his long black skirt pulled up around him as he held down his penis to relieve himself. Stunned and gasping for breath, Sister Teresa nearly fainted.

"Sister Alberta" got up off the commode in a flash, doubly relieved because no one besides the two of them was in the room. He pulled Sister Teresa aside and warned, "If you ever tell anyone about me, you will be very sorry, Sister!"

The overwhelmed nun could only stare at him horrified. Then she felt him grab her arm rather roughly as he led her to Room 101, the off-the-beaten-track room where the nuns went to have their hair cut short. There they could have a few minutes of privacy to talk since all the other nuns were still in the class that they had both left earlier only minutes apart.

"I'm so sorry I had to treat you the way I did back there, Teresa," "Sister Alberta" apologized as earnestly as "she" could.

By now Sister Teresa had retrieved her composure but still could only stare into the man/nun's eyes. Then she asked incredulously in a whisper, "Why are you doing this?"

"It's a long story, Teresa. Too long for now. We have to get back to vow class right away. Otherwise everyone will think we're up to something."

"Well, you certainly are. That's for sure!"

"I can't deny that, but you have to promise me you'll keep my secret until I explain why I'm doing this. I'll arrange a time and place soon. Promise me." "Sister Alberta" was now restraining Sister Teresa from leaving begging with his big browns for her to remain quiet.

In a whimper she replied, "Oh, all right!" leaving the room in a flash. At that "Sister Alberta" breathed a huge sign of relief, waited a few more minutes and then returned "herself" to the long room across from the Chapel where everyone was listening intently to Mother Evelyn's words. When he surreptitiously glanced across the table at Sister Teresa, her eyes were downcast, her demeanor blank. He hoped beyond hope she would keep her promise about his real identity.

Several nights later an hour after the Grand Silence at nine pm when no one was permitted to talk except in an emergency and then only in a doorway, Sister Teresa heard a soft knock at her cell door. She had been on the edge of sleep so at first she thought she was dreaming when she opened the door and "Sister Alberta" startled her by flowing into her arms. She closed the door as quickly as she could and stood completely shaken taken off guard. Later she would admit to herself that at first she felt they were burning through her long thin white nightgown into her very soul.

"Oh, Teresa," she heard him saying softly. "Thank you for keeping your promise."

Sister Teresa listened intently to "Sister Alberta's" plan as the two sat side by side on her single bed. As she did, she felt her insides rumbling mercilessly. Was this a dream or could it in any way be real? Should she just scream and get this man's charade out of the closet and into the light of day? Still she had given "Sister Alberta" her solemn promise to keep quiet and now he had explained why he was playing this dangerous game. So what should she do? Should she continue to keep quiet? Or should she go to Mother Evelyn and blow this man/nun's cover?

He was holding her hand now. As he squeezed it, he asked, "So are you with me or not, Teresa? Can you find it in your heart to help me for Sister Martha's sake?"

All Sister could get out of her mouth was a worried, "I don't know."

"But, Teresa, you were sent to help me, don't you understand that? A terrible wrong has been committed and I'm here to get some justice. I want Mother Evelyn who sent my dear friend to see that fiend of a priest who hurt her so badly and was an accessory to her death to pay!"

Finally, Sister Teresa got her voice back as she answered in querulous tones, "But how does turning the sisters and getting them to leave the convent do that?"

"Well, for one thing it will make your Mother Evelyn look like a complete failure. The community will question her leadership and she will be sent back to the ranks of the ordinary nuns defeated and distrusted."

"What I don't understand is why you didn't just go to the Bishop instead of coming here and tell him what Father Zachary did to Sister Martha."

"He wouldn't have believed me because he has such a good reputation and is about to become a Monsignor. He would have just thought I was out to destroy him."

"But wasn't that what you wanted from the beginning?"

"Only if I had proof which, of course, I don't now that Cindy is dead."

"But didn't you say there were others he hurt too?"

"My guess is a resounding yes, but again I don't have proof only rumors. My guess is the young nuns he's seduced have been too afraid to report him. He's a hero to the world. He does so much good. He's so honorable."

"I guess I get your point."

"It's getting really late. I don't want anyone to suspect us of anything. I'm leaving now, but we'll talk again. Sleep well, Teresa." At that he leaned over and kissed her softly on her lips. Then he disappeared like a wondrous image in a dream. The rest of the night Sister Teresa smiled in her sleep.

Life in the community continued as normal. Up at 6 am. Meditation and then the chanting of the Office of the Blessed Virgin and Mass at 7. Breakfast in silence. College classes. Prayers at noon before lunch when the good sisters could talk. More classes. Dinner at 5 again with conversation. Night Office of the Blessed Virgin followed by Study Hall at 7. Recreation at 8 with a sugar fix piece of chocolate except during Advent and Lent. Finally, the Grand Silence at 9 and bed by 10.

But for "Sister Alberta" and Sister Teresa that normalcy was gone. Over. Changed. All the young nun wanted was to be with "Sister Alberta." He came to her room almost every night at about ten, slipping into her bed and cuddling with her for the next hour or so until he felt sure he could slither down the hall to his cell without being seen by any of the other nuns who all dutifully fell asleep almost as soon as their heads hit their pillows shortly after the Grand Silence. The only one who routinely stayed awake hours later was Mother Evelyn who knew "Sister Alberta" was frequently slipping into Sister Teresa's cell. She never called them to task because she remembered all too well that when she was a new nun feeling especially homesick, she would go to a friend's bed just for the solace of another human being's body.

Sister Teresa glowed with the attention Ted gave her. She loved feeling his hands caress her body. For the first time in her twenty years, she believed someone truly cared about her. She lived each day only for the short time he was with her at night.

For himself "Sister Alberta" was falling fast in love with the gentle lovely nun. He had to work to restrain himself from being in her presence throughout the day for fear he'd be sent to Mother Evelyn for having what the nuns called "a particular friendship." Though no one ever said the word "lesbian" out loud, that was the latent fear of all the superiors especially for the young nuns. Of course, with contact essentially limited to women, it was no wonder that some did choose that route. "If they only knew what Teresa and I are really up to, they'd have their minds completely blown away!" Ted thought to himself repeatedly during the day and especially after 9 pm. Yes, he was falling in love with Teresa. As a result she was effectively ruining his Plan to destroy Mother Evelyn and the "good" Father. Still he couldn't deny his feelings for her and was sure she felt the same way about him.

He was right of course. Sister Teresa realized early on something very special was happening to her. "Sister Alberta" spoke to her in deep tones of respect and love. She would go to the ends of the Earth to be with him now so there was no way in the world she would ever divulge his plan to anyone.

Then one morning both of them became extremely nervous when Mother Evelyn called them to her office. Minutes later they were so relieved when she told "Sister Alberta" she was to be Sister Teresa's companion to go to the doctor's. Sister Teresa had said she hadn't been feeling up to par lately. Ironically, the two were to go to the same doctor who knew Ted's secret.

When Dr. Sam announced that Sister Teresa was pregnant, the couple was overwhelmed since they had only been with each other the whole way once. Apparently, that was enough.

At first all they could do was stare at each other, Sam shaking his head and Ted and Teresa frowning. How were they going to explain this turn of events to Mother Evelyn? There was really only one answer; the doctor would have to be Sister Teresa's cover. For her ongoing physical well being she would have to leave the confines of the convent on the East Coast and move to New Mexico to get relief from her extremely dangerous asthma condition.

So Sister Teresa wrote her letter of resignation to the Vatican and within a few weeks left the community to go West. "Sister Alberta" was not far behind her, leaving a month later to be on the safe side. She had explained in detail to Mother Evelyn that she was not suited for the religious life. She couldn't remain celibate. She wanted children. Mother Evelyn felt quite sad losing two more of her new nuns in addition to Sister Martha in such a short time but agreed with "Sister Alberta" that since she felt this way, she should leave the community and return to her other life in "the world."

What the upset superior never found out was that eight months later the former Sister Teresa delivered a healthy seven pound daughter into the arms of the former "Sister Alberta." That her happy parents named her Cynthia after Sister Martha. That Ted planned to tell his daughter when she became a teenager the strange story about how he and her mother met and how she was conceived. That Dr. Sam, who had left his practice in the East to live near them, agreed to be Cynthia's Godfather.

Ted's plan for retribution had, of course, gone by the wayside in the twists and turns of fate. Nevertheless, within the year after his darling little Cynthia was born, Mother Evelyn was removed from her position by her superiors since she was suspected of having an affair with the now Monsignor Zachary. Actually, she had broken off their long-time platonic relationship five months earlier in her concern that perhaps he had actually been getting it on with the young women she had sent to him for his help over the years.

One day shortly after "Sister Alberta" and Sister Teresa left the convent, Zachary admitted to Evelyn that he'd fallen again but didn't tell her with whom. Then the now simply "Sister Evelyn" remembered that Sister Mary Arthur had told her she thought Sister Martha was really shaken up after her first and only conference with Father Zachary. With a shock that vibrated throughout her body, Sister Evelyn realized what had actually happened to Sister Martha that day. Though horrified, she still couldn't let herself believe her friend had also taken advantage of the other young nuns she had sent to him in the past. One victim was too many, of course, but others as well? No way could "her" Zachary have descended that low!

Several weeks later Sister Evelyn heard through the hushed

words of another sister that Monsignor had been rushed to the hospital having suffered a heart attack. Later that day, Sister Evelyn stumbled into his room where she found him lifeless. She put her hand on his as his eyes ever so slightly opened. Zachary left this world whimpering, "Sorry... Sisters...." as the nun's tears washed over his ashen face.

PART II

What is Life but the living of it?
A Way of Awakening. A Dawn.
We wander far from ourselves
only to find it in us all along.

Elusive Peace

For the first time since he left the priesthood a quarter of a century ago, Ron McClancy, now married and the father of two teenage daughters, returned to his former monastery on the Pacific coast with his wife Annie. A die-hard atheist, absolutely certain there was no organizing intelligence in the Universe, she could never understand what had brought him at twenty-one to this out of the way place on top of a mountain. To this bizarre way of life. What's more what had unbelievably kept him in it for the next decade. Most of all, why he had to return here today.

None of the monks recognized Ron with his big paunch from indulging in the rich gourmet food of the wealthy. His premature white hair from his ongoing hassles with his irksome wife and spoiled daughters. His wrinkled brow from his constant worry about the money he would lose if the stock market ever took a nosedive and fell far south.

But Ron remembered most of the monks. Some with smiles to himself. Others with feelings of disdain. And for the new ones a sense of dismay and jealousy. His years at the monastery were generally difficult ones, yet when his current world closed in on him with all its problems, uncertainties and God awful noise, he longed to be here with the monks again relishing the silence, the beauty of the ocean and the mountains and the friendship of a certain few of the brothers.

Especially now with his marriage on the rocks and tasting more bitter than any drink he used to pretend he liked when he'd go out with the guys before he came here. Looking back with the hindsight of a man approaching fifty, he realized he married Annie on the run as the first woman he took an interest in right out of the monastery apparently because she was the antithesis of everything he used to believe in especially since she couldn't even accept that there was a God.

Today he wanted to be able to leave the chapel in procession with the monks once more and retreat to his cell where he would not be disturbed by phone calls from banks wanting him to refinance his house. Or knocks on the door by men asking if they could repave his driveway. Or faxes and emails and endless meetings. Or boring business trips to the middle of huge urban areas with no trees and impossible traffic jams.

But more than all of that, he wouldn't have to deal with Annie's incessant demands for attention especially in bed. It was too bad some couple's libidos didn't stay in sync with each other's throughout their marriages. Theirs certainly didn't. Annie simply did not interest him that way anymore. Yet the more he found reasons to put her off and keep her from trying everything in the book to turn him on, the more intent she was to have him. Thus, their circle of sexual discontent, frequently of late, had descended into angry frustration especially on her part. He knew he was hard pressed to keep on coping with her and all the many other disturbing challenges of "the world, the flesh, and the devil" for much longer. How that odd phrase jumped back into his consciousness after two decades, he didn't know.

As he sat listening to the haunting Georgian chant the monks were singing, he wondered if the community would take him back if he divorced Annie, took care of her and their two daughters' college financially, and then left them all. He doubted it, but he did know about a man who had been a missionary in South America for a quarter of a century who, when he returned to the states, left the priesthood to marry a woman in the parish where he was assigned. Only it didn't last. Unbelievably, he returned to the priesthood five years later. One of Annie's single friends had seen his ex at a Singles' Dance. More unbelievable was the subsequent turn of events. After he returned to the priesthood and became ill, she took care of him. Now if that wasn't truth stranger than fiction!

So what was he to do at this uncertain point in his life? Grin and bear his constantly complaining wife and daughters always wanting more money, more fashionable clothes, more lavish gifts? Nothing ever pleased them for longer than a few days like the ridiculously expensive vacation at a five star hotel in the islands last winter. The three of them were bored out of their minds in two days!

Today he nearly had to drag Annie "kicking and screaming" up this mountain to his former monastery. But now that they were here, he just wanted to leave. Without warning everything that upset him all those years ago fled back to him in a rush of heartburn, both figuratively and literally. The incessant "gnawing at his loins," as he referred to it all those years ago here, when he remembered late at night an attractive woman or a pretty girl he met at a Sunday dinner the monks shared with those staying in the trailers or motel like rooms of the monastery grounds for private retreats. The sanctimonious, hypocritical way some of the "holy" monks talked. The effeminate ways some of them acted. Their "old lady" bickering at chapter meetings. His own gnawing loneliness. Isolation. Discontent.

Then there was the institutional Church. As far as he was concerned, the current Powers that Be had turned Vatican II on its head leading the Church backward instead of forward into the twenty-first century by continuing to require priestly celibacy and refusing to ordain women. This despite how desperately they were needed to fill the ranks of priests like him who had left.

Out of the blue he remembered an extremely creative former nun named Marianna he met one Sunday many years ago at the shared dinner here. She had struck him as intuitive and insightful, full of adventure and fun. For all that still a holy woman who would have made a fine priest if she ever was given the chance or wanted it. "When the Pacific Ocean dries up and the sun turns to marmalade!" Ron chuckled to himself.

Just the thought of food even related to a long ago memory started making him feel sick now. He slipped out of the chapel as unobtrusively as he could and escaped to the nearby bathroom. The few breaths of fresh mountain air on the way down the sidewalk helped clear his head somewhat, but he knew it wasn't enough. He threw up his overpriced lunch of snails and champagne in the commode, his stomach heaving violently all the while. Still he didn't feel any better.

He'd have to explain at least some of the emotions he was feeling to Annie, but he didn't ever want to do that! No, he couldn't. He knew she'd never understand even if he tried.

He heard her voice now outside the door of the one person john calling out, "Are you all right in there, Ron?" Apparently she had followed him out of the chapel wondering where he was going all of a sudden though he knew she was certainly overjoyed with a reason as she would say "to get the hell out of that horrid place!" She had always been repulsed by all the trappings of a religion and a way of life she absolutely could never understand or accept.

"I'm fine. I'll be out in a few minutes." As Ron zipped his pants up, he almost laughed out loud thinking, "I wish I could zip that woman's God damn mouth up too!"

He just didn't want to face Annie. Didn't want to explain to her all the reasons why he had to come back here today. Then admit to her in the process all the mixed emotions about his past life clamoring for attention inside his soul as a result. When he opened the door, he saw her standing by their red Mercedes impatiently motioning for him to hurry. For now he had no other choice but to return to the other world of stock options, 401K's, mortgage payments, private school tuitions and, most of all, his unsettled life.

How Could She Have Known?

T he woman stood dumbfounded near the checkout line of the local supermarket. Someone had caught her attention in her right eye. She couldn't believe it. Why would a handsome young man half her age be staring at her? "I must be losing it," she thought to herself.

Turning back towards the checkout line with only a few items - peaches, grapes, plums and Greek yoghurt, she quickly forgot the man. As she waited for the cashier to ring up her purchases, she felt the presence of the man beside her. She spun around suddenly as he said, "Oh, you really are Mrs. Brandon, aren't you? Don't you remember me? I'm the guy you always caught smoking back in high school. The one everyone thought would never go anywhere."

The woman smiled courteously, quickly flipping through the

memory files of her brain, but nothing about this handsome young man/former student registered.

As she continued to smile at the stranger, he announced, "I went into computers when I graduated. I hated it at first but the company I started years ago is doing rather well. I'm the CEO." Then a glint in his eye as he said, "We're connected with Facebook."

He paused for a moment looked behind him and then whispered in her ear, "I'm also a millionaire."

The woman barely blinked as she picked up her groceries, smiled goodbye and wished the man continued success.

What she couldn't have known was that this student she didn't remember was really an inveterate liar. He currently was on probation for assaulting a woman, had only a hundred dollars to his name and didn't even own a computer.

The Woman in the Winery

On a road trip to Santa Barbara on the California coast, a woman barely beyond middle-aged named Nora and her son Barry, a handsome tall twenty-two year old, stopped by an off-the-beaten-track winery. As soon as they stepped into the tiny store and wine tasting room, a grey haired woman just a few years younger than Nora smiled warmly at Barry from behind the counter.

"How may I help you today, Sir?" she cooed.

"Nothing right now, thanks," Barry responded, unaware of the special attention the woman was giving him.

"Look around all you want, Hon. You just let me know if there's any way I can help you." Then she turned around and Nora noted she gulped what seemed like half a glass of red wine before she turned around again smiling in Barry's direction. Her eyes followed him as he looked at bottles of wine and decanters and designer socks on the shelves. Nora couldn't get over how blatantly the woman stared at her son trying to engage him. Still he remained oblivious of her attention the whole time the two of them were in the store.

When the mother and her son left after several sips of wine, the shopkeeper took another long gulp of the grape before walking over to the door and watching their car drive off down the road. Then she bit her lip and sat down on the tall stool behind the counter and cried.

In the car Nora laughed as she told her son what she had just witnessed. "Didn't you notice how that woman in that shop kept coming on to you?"

"What? Of course not."

"Come on, Barry. You must know you're a good looking guy."

"Whatever, Mom."

"Well, it looks like we're almost at our little inn in the woods."

"That's good news."

Back at the wine shop, the woman dried her eyes and locked the door. She really didn't want to go home, but she knew she had to. She had hoped the half bottle of wine she drank in the past hour would buoy her up for the inevitable task of facing her husband tonight. Still she knew that nothing, not even her innocent flirtation with the handsome young guy who had just come into the shop, could sustain her in advance.

She only had to walk across the path behind the store and in front of the vineyard to get to her house. She gritted her teeth as she turned the knob and walked into the foyer hoping Stan would be asleep, but no such luck. He was up and ready to pounce on her.

"So what have you been doing all this frigging afternoon? I've been over here starving!" Stan snarled at her from his wheelchair. His face was red, his eyes dark, his fist shaking in her direction. Louise knew if he had had something hard in his hand like a dish or a cup or even a cell phone, he might have thrown it at her.

"Now, Honey.... I..."

"Don't try to placate me, Louise! I know you stay over at that damn store way beyond hours so you don't have to...."

"But I left you a bowl of soup on the table that you could heat in the microwave. Also some crackers, cheese and fruit."

"So you think that was enough to get me through the whole damn day? A stinking bowl of bean soup you know I hate and some stale crackers and cheese and two nearly rotten peaches. Sickening!"

Louise knew there was no way to calm her husband down. She also knew all too well that instead of eating what she left for him, he had just lunched on a bottle of vodka. Though she didn't see the bottle, his words and actions told her loud and clear that he'd been drinking a lot and she was in for it. Tonight was certainly not going to be pleasant or peaceful.

"So what do you have to say for yourself, damn it! Were you over there all day making eyes at every young guy who came in? I know you. Desperate for any little taste of fun. Any little taste of forbidden pleasure. You are disgusting!" Stan slumped in his chair mumbling to himself for the next few moments apparently worn out from his tirade.

Louise dumped the soup down the garbage disposal along with the crackers and cheese that had been sitting out on the kitchen table all afternoon. Then she threw the peaches in the trash. There was no way she could force herself to eat dinner, let alone cook anything for Stan, but she knew she'd better or else. She pulled out a frozen chicken and vegetable combo from the freezer and literally tossed it into the microwave. As soon as her husband jerked awake in a few minutes, she'd have it ready for him. She sank down on a kitchen chair, her head in her hands.

Before she realized what was happening, Stan wheeled his chair right up behind her, yanked a bunch of her hair aside and yelled in her ear, "You disgusting piece of meat, I want you out of here! You aren't going to serve me some frozen piece of crap for dinner. I'd rather not eat at all. And you'll be responsible when they find me starved to death by my own wife! Now get out! NOW!"

"But Stan...."

"NOW, damn it!" He started looking frantically for something to throw at her.

Louise was so scared and agitated she proceeded to drop the contents of the frozen dinner all over the already dirty floor. As some hunting magazines began to fly at her, she grabbed her purse, slammed the front door and ran to her car. Stan was acting worse than she'd ever remembered lately. Not knowing what else to do, she sped to the inn down the road. Fortunately, they had a room available for the night. She fell into the bed in her clothes and cried herself to sleep.

Early the next morning she woke angry and desperate. What should she do? If something happened to Stan, she'd be responsible.

Distraught, she had to clear her mind.

As she sat staring into space drinking a steaming mug of black caffeine, she happened to notice someone she recognized across the room. It was that young man from yesterday sitting over by the window with that older woman. Yeah, they were strangers, but she was in such a bind, she thought maybe they could help her somehow.

"Excuse me, I know this is odd, but..."

Nora and Barry both looked up, remembering her as the woman they had talked about.

"You don't look well. What's wrong?" Nora replied, her eyes looking warily at the woman.

"Well, you see, my husband...."

"Is he ill? Do you need me to call a doctor or...."

"No, Stan threw me out of the house last night...."

"Really?"

"Oh, it's all so terrible! You see, I'm to blame for the condition he's in. Five years ago he slipped on the wax I had just put down on the kitchen floor. He's completely paralyzed as a result and now he drinks an awful lot of vodka all the time and... and...." Louise started to break down as tears flowed down her face.

Nora and Barry sat stunned. What could they do for this poor stranger? Barry got up and brought her a glass of water. Louise thanked him through her tears smiling weakly. Then she continued, "Forgive me, but I lost my only son Zack because of all of this too. My husband convinced him I wanted him dead so my dearest boy believed him and enlisted in the god damn Army. Oh, excuse me. Well last month we got a letter stating he was killed by a roadside bomb in Iraq." Now Louise's wails began to ring out through the breakfast area. Other patrons turned around abruptly to stare at her for a moment and then continued eating, but Nora and Barry sat motionless waiting until the woman got hold of herself. Nora handed her a wad of tissues, pulling her down into the seat beside her.

"I'm so sorry, but I don't know your name."

"Louise. Louise Timons."

"Well I'm Nora Baker and this is my son Barry. We'll try to help you in any way we can. First, you've got to eat something. Barry, why don't you fix a plate for Louise?"

"Sure thing, Mom. Back in a sec."

Nora watched Louise watch Barry as he strode across the room. She knew now why she was smiling at him earlier and whom he reminded her of.

"Louise, isn't there any one in the area you can talk to or stay with? We could drive you wherever you need to go."

"Unfortunately, there's no one. I don't have any family or friends in the area. I spend all my time taking care of Stan and the vineyard and, of course, the shop. I don't know where to go or what to do."

"First things first, Louise. You eat some breakfast and then we'll think of something."

Louise realized just how hungry she was, not having eaten anything since lunch the day before. When Barry put the plate of pancakes and fresh fruit in front of her, she ate hurriedly afraid that at any minute Stan was going to wheel up behind her and yell at her to do something for him. Of course, she knew she had left him at their house to fend for himself when he threw her out. Maybe she should call or get someone to go and check on him. Perhaps Barry would.

"Nora, I'm wondering. Do you think your son might go by the house and see if Stan's all right? I know he'll just yell at me and get madder than anything if I try to check on him."

"Oh, I don't know if that's such a good idea, Louise, Barry being a stranger and all."

"But you said you'd help me. Oh please, Barry, will you do this for me?"

Even though Nora was shaking her head "No," Barry smiled and said, "OK, Mrs. Timons. Let's all drive to your house, and I'll look in on him for you."

When Barry came back to Louise's car after only a few minutes in her house, his face was ashen and drawn. Louise cried out, "What's the matter, Barry? What happened in there? Did my husband threaten you? Please say he didn't!"

"No, he didn't do anything to me. In fact, he didn't even seem to see me. I guess you won't believe this, but he was doing jumping jacks in the den! I left as soon as I saw him."

"Wait, Barry, what do you mean? Stan can't walk. He's confined to a wheel chair!"

"Maybe then it wasn't Stan I saw. Is there anyone else who might have been in your house?"

"No, I can't imagine who. Was the man you saw working out about 6'2" with dark brown hair probably wearing grey sweat pants and a T-shirt?"

"Yeah."

"I don't understand. How could he.... Oh no, he's been lying to me ever since.... and my son lost his life because of..." Louise banged her head on the steering wheel sobbing. When she stopped, she smiled ruefully and screamed, "Why I could kill him, that repulsive Son of a Bitch, he's ruined my life!"

Nora got out of her car and walked over. "What's the matter? What happened? Are you two all right?"

"Yes, Mom. But Mrs. Timons' husband... Apparently, he's not really paralyzed. I saw him standing up doing exercises."

"Oh, Dearest Lord in Heaven. What are you going to do Louise?"

Louise had no words. All she wanted to do was grab Stan, pummel him to the floor and hurt him even half as much as he had hurt her. But she felt defeated. Worthless. Spent. She simply had no fight left in her body.

Nora realized that the woman was probably going into shock. "Take it easy, Louise. Come with us. We'll drive you to the police station down the road. Maybe you can get a restraining order against your husband. He's been abusing you for some time, hasn't he?"

From somewhere in her disturbed body, Louise whimpered a small, "Yes."

Nora helped her out of her car and into hers. Within the next few hours she managed to set up the restraining order. Nora then insisted that they all stay at a different hotel in the next town that night where Stan most likely wouldn't be able to find them.

In the meantime Stan was going ballistic at the house. Throwing vases of flowers and plants at the wall. Kicking furniture over. Pushing his wheelchair down the cellar stairs. Then rushing outside and pulling up vines in the vineyard by their roots. That's where the police found him to deliver the R.O. He took a cursory look at the paper, swore vociferously and attempted to punch out one of the detectives. When he missed, he sank to the ground still spewing curses at the officers. The deputy then read him his rights, cuffed him and drove him away in the squad car. The next morning the guard found him babbling like a baby as he stood on his head against the bars of his cell. Days later he was ordered to undergo a psychiatric evaluation.

When Louise was told that Stan was certifiable and was to be institutionalized, she hurried to her new friends' room and hugged Nora and her son goodbye promising them she'd stay in touch. Then the police dropped her at her house where she packed a suitcase for Stan and began to clean the house. When she saw her husband's mangled wheelchair at the bottom of the stairs, she curled up in a fetal position on the cold kitchen floor and sobbed like a lost little girl.

The Confession

Thrusting himself into the seat beside her, the burly man gave Jan the irksome sense that he had singled out that place from all the other vacant ones on the bus. She didn't want to be trapped into talking to anyone during this part of her trip. "Why this seat? Why here?" she complained to herself. After all, she had just wasted the past hour and a half in a disturbing discussion about Vietnam with a guy recently out of an Army stockade supposedly for having been involved in a My Lai type incident. At the first rest stop Jan had luckily gotten out of going for coffee with him by staying in the ladies' room until the last minute.

Now she saw the soldier climbing back on the bus. As he passed his already occupied seat, she tried to communicate a silent, "I couldn't help it," but he just shook his head disgustedly as he pushed past her to find another place somewhere behind her.

In an annoying way the man now beside Jan squirmed in his seat. His restless movements seemed to keep repeating, "Talk to me.

Talk to me," but Jan ignored him burying herself even deeper into the novel for her Masters she had vowed to read on this lap of her trip to graduate school for a thesis conference with her advisor.

She had only read several chapters when squealing and screeching brought her back to the bus from the intrigues of Isabel in Portrait of a Lady. Now the aggravating man next to her was playing a game of some sort with the two little boys across the aisle. "Only another ploy to get my attention," Jan complained to herself. "Why can't this guy get the message that I'm not interested in him?" She simply didn't want to talk to anyone, least of all to him. "Men can be so dense at times," she almost said out loud. Then she continued reading.

About fifteen minutes later the man beside her announced, "Get ready. I'm going to take off my coat now!" Jan reluctantly glanced over at him; he was smiling at her in that certain ingratiating way she had always despised in men. Actually his expression was more of an outright smirk - the kind that really turned her off, irrationally perhaps, yet absolutely nevertheless.

"So what's your problem? A hang-up about talking to strange men?"

Jan sat silent.

"For the love of God, lady, at least you could answer yes or no. Do me that one little honor, will ya?"

Without really wanting to, Jan resigned herself to the inescapable situation and responded, "I just want to read. Do you mind?"

"Of course I mind. A guy gets on a bus, sees an empty seat next to a good-looking dame and decides that's the best place for him. Got some problem with that?"

"Well, no, not exactly. It's just that..."

"Hey, either you and me talk like two civilized people sitting beside each other on a long bus trip or we don't. But don't get me wrong. I'm not begging you to talk to me. Still, since we're both stuck here together for at least another hour or so, why don't we make the best of it? Hell, who knows, you might find out I have something to say. Or then again, maybe even you do."

At this point the man's head shot back as a hearty laugh roared out of his mouth. In spite of her previous resolve, Jan heard herself say, "OK, you win. My name's Janet. What's yours?"

"So you want to know my name, do ya? I'd say that's a little forward for such a quiet..."

"Shy would be a better word."

"Sure, sure, my mother always told me to watch out for you shy ones. You're the ones to be careful of."

"Perhaps you're right."

"You bet I am, babe. I've been around. Known lots of different kinds of broads."

"So what kind of work do you do?"

"Business in Panama. I'm just back in the states for a taste of 'R and R', you might say. How about you?"

"I'm a teacher... high school English."

"What? An English teacher? I don't believe it. I never was any good at all that reading and writing crap. Was lucky I got out of high school. Hmm, and you're not married either. I always make a point of checking. Avoid a lot of bad deals that way. So you've got all the makings of an old maid except for the looks. Hell, I don't get it. What is your thing? How come no guy's hitched up with you yet? And don't go giving me that too shy excuse."

"No, it's not that at all. I just haven't met the right man yet. That's why." Jan bit her tongue as this trite excuse flowed out of her mouth like syrup on her weekend waffles.

"Still can't believe it, you being such a good looker and all. Say, you should come to Panama. The women I know there are really something else. They sure swing! Lots of us men for them all, too. By the way, mind if I hit you with another personal question?"

"All right if you have to," Jan replied reluctantly.

"Honestly now, weren't you really glad when I got on the bus and sat down here beside you?"

"Ummm... actually I... that is, no, I wasn't."

"That does it! You are something else, woman! I thought so when I first spied you and now I'm really convinced! But, oh hell, what's the use of arguing? Let's get back to Panama. Like I was saying, the women I know there are all really winners. Especially this one chick. She's really a broad and a half. Wants me to marry her and all that but I just can't see it. Piece of ass now and then is enough for me. And what a good piece she is! Outstanding! Met her at one of those cocktail parties. Long blond hair and what legs! To boot it all, at least a 40 D! She's really 'out of sight' as they say."

Jan's stomach churned. What did she care about this guy and his woman? The whole story was simply disgusting. How she hated being trapped next to this jerk! There wasn't any doubt in her mind; liquor had loosened his tongue beyond her endurance. "Well, he'll be sorry," she vowed to herself.

He continued rambling on, words jumping out of his mouth as if gasping hungrily for air. "There ain't no broads like that one around here that's for sure. She can really turn me on. But none of them wedding bells for this guy. I like to eat my cake and have it too. Get that play on words, Teach? Pretty good pun, eh?"

At that the man beside Jan roared another embarrassingly loud belly laugh as she grimaced unabashedly. Oblivious to her reaction, the man did, however, soften his voice to a somewhat more restrained bellow and then continued, "Say, I bet I could give you some real good pointers on how to land a guy since you're still out there looking. First off, get yourself an overseas job. Lots more men and fun for you over there. Just remember them eyes. Sounds funny, but they're key those eyes. Man always knows what kind of woman he's talking to by her eyes. Let 'em talk to tell him you want him to light your fire and turn you on. No doubt about it, some broads really can show the hots they have for you just by the way they look at you. Can give a guy a hard on right on the spot, if you know what I mean."

At this point Jan could only volunteer a weak, "Hmmm." Disgust was surging wildly within her. Her stomach churned. Bile rose in her throat. She knew she couldn't take this obnoxious verbal man's abuse too much longer. One thing was sure. If she told him about herself, he'd be sorry.

"Eyes. Yes, sir, the eyes," he kept repeating. "Sock it to 'em, baby. Sock it to... Hey, wait a minute. Wait a minute. You know something, you are just too damn quiet. By now after all this time you should have let me have it straight. But you just want to play it cool. I

know your kind. Want me to lay on all the compliments and butter you
up real good. Well, babe, that's not going to happen! No, sir, Bud don't
bow down to no broad. They give him the come on first or else I just
bug off, see?"

To this Jan wanted to retort, "Then why don't you? I never even
wanted to talk to you in the first place!" but she bit her lip instead and
remained silent. Her confession would take care of everything. Yes, it
was the best thought she'd come up with to do something about the man
beside her. She'd tell him all right. Her announcement will quiet him
down and maybe even shut him up for good. She smiled to herself as
she waited for the right moment to tell him. Under these irksome
circumstances it couldn't come soon enough.

Despite her silence, the man beside her refused to give up.
"Hey, baby, I bet you could be really interesting to get to know. I mean
really become intimate and all that. So what do you say? Maybe we
could get together some time. You could sign up for Panama. We'd
have one hell of a great time - you and me! One hell of a swinging
time, I guarantee you! Good whiskey, wine, beer. Lots of laughs.
Plenty of fun and games!" Again he laughed without restraint.

"He really thinks he's going to win me over, but wait until he
finds out," Jan said to herself and inadvertently laughed out loud.

"There you go, doll, that's better. Go ahead, relax and enjoy.
You're too up tight for your own good. Just take it easy and go on
laughing. Me and you are really going to go places together."

He started talking even louder at this point. Jan reddened as
new waves of overwhelming embarrassment surged furiously
throughout her body. Certainly the other passengers couldn't help but

overhear the man's obnoxious comments and obscene laughs.

"So, come on, baby doll, what's the good word, eh?"

Jan sat silent.

"Ah, shit! You are without a doubt one hell of a damn stubborn broad! Just what is your problem? Jesus Christ, you must be some kind of weirdo!"

Now the man's sneering bellows echoed even louder up and down the aisles of the bus. Again Jan winced. "He's the one who's too much!" she thought. What a repulsive show he was putting on for everyone, all at her expense. She could only imagine what her previous seat mate was thinking about her now.

Then the man swore again, "God damn it! How's a guy supposed to enjoy a bus ride with a crazy broad like you beside him? Hell, I would have done better with some gay guy."

Pursing her lips, Jan angrily jerked toward the man and looked directly into his glassy bloodshot eyes for the first time. Then as casually as she could, she asked, "How securely are you seated in your seat?"

His usual blustery laugh preceded his nonchalant reply. "Fine. Just fine, Lady. No question about me. You're the one with the problem."

Jan shook her head, "I... I have something to tell you... something you should know. I... " she swallowed hard and continued resolutely, "I'm... I'm a nun."

Silent at last, the man could now only stare horrified at the girl/ woman/nun beside him as though she had just delivered a powerful punch below his belt knocking the wind out of him. She had the sense then that if he could have, he would have jumped through the floor of the bus to disappear.

Uneasy now, Jan almost immediately regretted that she had said anything. If only she had kept her mouth shut. If only she had just let him ramble on and on. Surely, she could have somehow managed to keep on swallowing her embarrassment to be more civil about his annoying behavior.

But then again, no! He deserved to be shut up! It was all his fault anyway; she didn't ask him to sit next to her. She didn't encourage him to tell her how to pick up men or how to be such a grand sexual success. He had been rude and obnoxious beyond her endurance.

A somewhat subdued yet angry voice from the man interrupted her thoughts. "Damn it, Lady, nun, or whoever you really are, you think you're smart, don't you? Waiting until I get into things so deep that I bury myself. Some good joke but it won't work. Why I ought to..." His voice trailed off as though someone had just levied another quick punch in his groin.

Then he stopped short and demanded, "Wait one God damn minute, Little Lady! Tell me just one thing. Are you or aren't you putting me on? You a nun living in a nunnery with no men to get it on with? How do you expect me to believe that? Your hair's showing and your legs, too. And what about that fancy coat you're wearing? You've got to be shitting me, oops, I mean..."

Shaking her head slowly, Jan found herself replying softly, "No, I... I... you just have to believe me. Some nuns wear regular clothes now."

"So I'm supposed to believe you're a nun just because you say so? No way! Sure, you caught me off guard but, but no one puts Bud Saylor down, least of all an odd broad like you!" He glared a threat at her, pounding his hairy fist angrily on the armrest between them.

Now Jan squirmed even more uncomfortably in her seat. Wouldn't she ever get rid of this maniac beside her? Wasn't there any way to shut him up?

When the bus finally jerked to a stop, she watched the disgruntled man beside her push himself into the surging line headed toward the door. No, he had not believed her. She should have tried lesbian.

He was waiting for her when she got off the bus with one final question, "Why couldn't you have been just some ordinary woman I met on a bus?" Jan didn't have an answer. Shaking her head, she walked away.

Joy's Esperanza

For almost forty years Joy had been telling her new literature students each semester some of the things she has learned about life. Specifically, that truth was stranger than fiction. That art imitates life imitating art. That life is an ongoing circle of the strange versus the real as well as the actual versus the fantastic. She never thought she would have to live those lines.

One day in her late 60's when she found out she had one last egg that had been fertilized, she gasped in shock. "How can this be, Doctor? There hasn't been a man in my life for the past ten years. No one since a fool named Dexter who lived up to his name as 'King of My Heart,' but then abdicated his throne when he found himself a young princess. Furthermore, I went through menopause more than a quarter of a century ago!"

Joy stared at her doctor, dismay and disbelief scratched across her face. "I just can't wrap my mind around this reality. Did I sleepwalk into someone's bed? How in the world could one of my eggs have survived and be viable enough to be...?"

"Well, perhaps it was that shot of testosterone I gave you last month or some test tubes were switched accidentally... But no, that can't be. I can't really explain this. Let's just wait and see how things go. Before you leave, line up another appointment with me for a month from today."

"But, Doctor, I can't be..."

"Now, Joy, go home now and take a nice hot bath and relax. Everything's going to work out. There is a line in the *Desiderata* that goes, 'Whether or not it is clear to you, no doubt the universe is unfolding as it should.'"

Later that afternoon, Joy ran herself a steamy tub adding an extra amount of her favorite lavender bath salts to it. As she soaked, she wondered to whom she could tell her unbelievable news. Her daughters Betty and Tina? No, they had too much on their plates with roaming-eyed husbands. Her son James? No, he was too wrapped up in his retail business. Her best friend Arlene? No, she'd never believe this pregnancy could possibly be true. She'd just think she was making up one of her usual farfetched stories so no use telling her. No, there really wasn't anyone.

But if her Don was still alive, how joyous he'd be, though overwhelmed, of course, as well. Relaxing more and more completely in the velvety water, Joy let herself relive the day fifty years ago when she found out she was pregnant for the first time with their only son James. Ah, what a pleasant memory meeting Don afterwards and reveling in the good news together.

Joy slowly started to bathe herself now as she tried to accept the overwhelming reality of her unique current condition. For some strange reason she felt aligned to the universe and realized she was being primed for something momentous by forces beyond and outside her control.

Then inexplicably from somewhere deep inside herself she heard the words, "This being you are carrying is the Child of Yourself. It will flow out when the time is right. All there is now is the Waiting. Then the Coming. The Greeting. The Loving."

As she listened, Joy felt herself glowing excessively warm with this awareness. A hot flash during her pregnancy with the Child of Herself? On some stranger–than-fiction level it all made sense. Or did it? She was incredulous. "Carrying the 'Child of Myself' at nearly seventy and having hot flashes at the same time? Imagine!"

Then she reasoned she needed a name for this child whoever it was and wherever it came from without any input from a father or any seemingly viable egg from her. She still couldn't understand how she somehow became fertile enough in her advanced years to become a mother again.

All at once the name "Esperanza" came to her deepest self out of the lovely blue of the morning sky. A perfect name "Esperanza:" the embodiment of Hope in the future despite the raging inner and outer wars she faced every day.

"Esperanza. Esperanza. The Child of Myself. Of my new life. The rest of my life!" Joy gloried in the idea and then crazily asked herself, "When is a clone not a clone?" and even answered, "When it's a koan."

"Nonsensical!" she chided herself. "How silly I'm getting. How long I've been on this earth and only now pregnant with the Child of Myself!"

After stepping out of the tub, she celebrated her awareness of the new life inside her by dancing across the room in circle after circle. Then she remembered a spiritual Sufi dance at a consciousness workshop she attended years before as well as "The Happening" she staged with her speech class many, many years earlier. Always flowing, spinning, gyrating, laughing... Such wonderful experiences!

Suddenly, a throbbing pain at the top of her right leg jerked her out of her nostalgic memories reminding her that "Arty," as she called the vexing condition, was still out to get her. In the grand scheme of things, it was a minor scourge for her to suffer compared to other truly debilitating or ultimately terminal conditions some of her friends suffered. Nevertheless, sometimes Arty's thrust of pain almost made her lose her balance and fall.

"Still," she continued to herself, "scientists are now projecting we could live decades beyond a hundred. If it's taken almost seventy years for this Child of Myself to get ready to be born, then hopefully I'll have a lifetime afterwards, perhaps an additional fifty years to get to know her." At that she chided herself again for harboring such ridiculous thoughts.

Her mind jerked back and forth from the fantasy of such a long double life to the reality of what was supposedly mysteriously developing inside her womb. She wondered, "Will this being need another seven decades to be born? Oh, what's really happening to me? Am I going out of my mind or what?"

"Miss Joy... Miss Joy. I'm finished. Feel free to relax here for as long as you want. Remember to drink lots of water today. Bye now. Be well."

I whimpered a weak, "Thank you, Meghan," as I lay nearly unconscious on the heated massage table. It would take me many minutes to return fully to this room and to my certainly non-pregnant self. And, more importantly, many days, months and years to comprehend the full meaning of my experience in the parallel universe I was transported to as my masseuse worked my weary arthritic body into complete relaxation and renewed peace.

As I left the room, I remembered a line from Erich Fromm, "Man's main task in life is to give birth to himself, to become what he potentially is."

Adrift

"All significant battles are waged within ourselves." Anon.

They saw each other for the first time across the Calypso Bar on the cruise ship to the Eastern Caribbean as soon as they each sat down. Both were alone.

She noted his warm smile when he glanced over at her and especially his full head of curly black hair. "No guy should have hair that beautiful!" she complained to herself. Hers was always so straight and thin; she never minded getting it cut.

He sensed she was shy and reserved but trying to put on a good show that she wasn't. Her smile in response to his just barely peeked out of the corners of her mouth. He knew there was something definitely different about her; he just couldn't put his finger on what that elusive something was. She certainly wasn't the typical woman sitting alone at a bar on a cruise ship. From his vantage point she looked almost dowdy wearing a plain white top and no jewelry except a silver bracelet on her left arm. Her short brown hair was cut straight just above her ears. She seemed like a delicate flower someone picked and forgot about in the Calypso bar in the middle of the ocean. She just didn't fit the scene.

As he kept trying to figure her out, she was continuing to do the same for him. What she noticed from her surreptitious glances across the bar were his ringless finger on his left hand, his light blue shirt and beige jacket and an oddly appealing five o'clock shadow on his handsome face. He intrigued her but she knew full well that there was no way she could imagine ever talking to him.

But what if they did connect somehow? What would happen then? As she sipped her white wine spritzer, she let her imagination wander....

She saw herself standing alone on the uppermost deck of the ship staring far out into the endless midnight ocean. Suddenly, she felt a cool hand caress her neck. Her intuition told her it was him - the intriguing man from across the bar! She turned and smiled into his hazel eyes. Oh, he was so fine! Then they walked hand in hand around and around the ship. They didn't need to talk. The friendly pressure of his hand on hers was more than enough for her. For how many years she had yearned for the wondrous feelings now ebbing through her body....

"Miss. Miss! Here's your check. Are you OK? You seem so..."

"Oh, I'm sorry. Yes, yes, I'm fine," Mary Alice mumbled, stirred abruptly out of her romantic reverie by the multiple earringed bartender.

She signed the receipt, smiling weakly at the young blond haired man and then swirled around in her stool. Just as she did, the handsome man she had noticed from across the bar walked by. As she felt his body accidentally press against hers, her face raged hot and turned crimson. Caught off guard, she was so discombobulated she could only squeak out a faint "Sorry."

The man smiled his inimitable smile she had already noted and responded, "Well, I'm certainly not!"

Mary Alice jerked away from him, now even more embarrassed. Her heart was beating so fast and furious, she was certain the stranger could hear it pounding like a hundred steel drums inside her. She was so irked at herself! She had worked so hard at fitting in and not standing out. Trying to be like every other woman on the ship. And now not only had she been attracted from afar to this handsome man, she had fallen right into his arms for everyone at the bar to notice!

Though there was no way she could have believed it possible, James was totally enthralled with her. She wasn't like any other woman he had ever met or worked with. When she nearly fell into his arms, it was the best shock of his life and so overwhelming pleasant, he couldn't find words in his head to describe how good her body felt against his. He hoped she wasn't offended by how his lower body - his "third leg" as some jokingly called it - reacted almost immediately. What a way to meet such a very different woman!

For a few moments it seemed like time stopped for both

travelers. They couldn't move apart. They couldn't look away from each other's eyes. It was as though an umbilical cord had mysteriously bonded them together.

Then as quickly as they connected as it were outside time and space in some parallel universe, the ship lurched slightly and the connection between them was nearly broken.

Neither one could have ever guessed the background or the current circumstances of the other as they stood by the bar of the ship overwhelmed by the strong emotions of their accidental encounter....

James O'Malley grew up in a wealthy, extremely religious Catholic family in Central Indiana. He always felt his fate was determined from the day of his First Communion when he was eight years old. His uncle - a Monsignor - said the Mass whispering in his ear as he gave him the host, "You are meant to serve God, Jimmy." Five years later James woke up one day in a seminary. Everything had happened so fast it was as though he was caught in a whirlwind which as much as propelled him to that place. His parents were ecstatic. His friends in dismay. He was shell shocked. He couldn't believe what he had actually done. He was only thirteen and away from home for the first time. What did he know of the world? Yet, like the proverbial lamb to the slaughter, he stayed behind those walls though never fully understanding why or how he got there and never totally accepting it or admitting that fact to anyone beside himself. Years passed and he was ordained a priest. Still under his robes at Mass and frequently elsewhere, he was in constant turmoil, never fully buying into all it meant to be dedicated to this life especially to celibacy.

Now he was already thirty-five, an assistant pastor of a suburban parish on a vacation for the first time in his life, thanks to a special birthday gift from a group of his parishioners. On his own. Alone. Free of all responsibilities. Anonymous. And it felt so damn good! That is until the woman at the bar turned on her stool and as much as fell into his arms as he walked by her at the same time. Yes, until then he was fine. Now how would he handle this sudden new challenge?

He was in a panic wanting her. Yearning to take her in his arms and feel her smooth skin against his hungry body. Laugh with her. Share himself with her. Take her for all she was worth in body and soul. Yet he didn't have a clue how any of this could ever possibly happen....

Mary Alice McGrogan, on the other hand, grew up on the wrong side of the tracks in a small town in Ohio. Her nearly indigent Catholic parents offered her little chance to be able to leave the area. They certainly had no money to send her to college. Like a ship inexorably borne out to sea in a storm, in a desperation move for all the wrong reasons, she found herself at eighteen a new nun called a postulant in a religious community thirty miles away. Once there her whole standard of living improved from lower to middle class. Still she had to deal with incessant bouts of homesickness as well as constant penances and self denials so she really didn't get her subsequent college degree for free. Years later she would realize just how much she had actually paid for that education with her self esteem shred in tatters and her femininity and even her personhood in disarray as well.

One day in her late twenties she woke up and decided she had to take a taste of the world before she made a major decision to stay or to leave the convent which she intuitively knew was actually a decision to leave or to stay herself. During the time she was teaching at a boarding school for teenage girls, she came up with a Plan. She borrowed some clothes from a new friend, the lay physical education teacher of the school, who even paid for the ticket for the cruise. She as much as pushed Mary Alice out the door after she told her superior that she was visiting a sick family friend for the week.

Everything was going along without a hitch on the cruise until she swung around on her bar stool too fast and fell right into the arms of the handsome man she had previously noticed sitting across the room from her. Now what was she going to do? How would she handle what she was feeling for the first time in her life thanks to him? How was she to cope with the new urges stirring in her body? Ones she couldn't explain or understand because her superiors had never adequately prepared her for them. All Mary Alice knew was she wanted to touch that handsome man, hold him, caress him and laugh and talk to him. She was so out of the sexual loop she didn't know about doing anything else. Her wildest dream was simply to be with him....

∽ ⁀

Sister Mary Alice's meditation book slid out of her hands onto the floor of the chapel just as Father James came out on the altar for the daily Mass. As she retrieved it, a flash of the fine dream she had just dreamt when she dozed off during meditation in the warm chapel a half hour ago made her catch her breath. She smiled for a few moments indulging herself again in her impossible but nevertheless wondrous fantasy. She knew all too well that only in her vivid imagination could she live a double life without a double commitment. Having the actual "Man of Her Dream" without ever having him though she had no idea what really "having him" meant.

Realistically, there was no possible future she could imagine for the man and the woman in her dream. No, they were fated to remain apart adrift and alone.

In her waking life, though, she would see him at least on the altar each morning at Mass and at other times when she helped him with home Masses for invalids and Sunday Masses for the teens at the local juvenile detention center. She was certain he had no idea whatsoever about what she imagined the two of them could be in her fantasy world. And what's more, he could never know! She could never tell him. If she did, he'd probably only laugh and ask, "What can I say?" Then he'd smile his inimitable fine smile as though it was all a joke. No, she could never, ever let that happen! She couldn't let herself risk losing even the few hours she actually had with him as part of the responsibilities of her vocation. Her resolve was firm. This was the way it had to be and that was that.

But how she wished in every fiber of her being that it didn't have to be that way. She wanted something wonderful to change everything. Baring that, she tried to reassure herself that at least she had her cruise dream. That would have to be enough. That would have to sustain her in a life she still questioned yet didn't have the guts or the nerve to get up and leave.

One thing she couldn't make herself accept was an intuitive

insight that he, too, was questioning everything in his life. That he was interested in her as a man is in a woman and as a result yearn for her as a man. No, that could never be! She could never let her imagination run away with her mind like that. She couldn't let herself even think he could ever want her. And more, that he could ever see in her anything even to want. The brainwashing of her superiors over the years had worked very well.

Looking out over the congregation as he delivered the homily, ironically on love and commitment, Father James thought his eye caught Sister Mary Alice's. It was a fleeting glance at best but enough to rattle him to his bones momentarily. He wondered if he'd ever resolve his ambivalent feelings about remaining celibate....

Since there was so much these two dedicated people would never know about each other or be able to resolve about the life choices they had made, they remained adrift and apart for the rest of their lives.

Who Fell Off the Roof?

Every time Suzy and her Mom and Dad and little sister visited Grandma and Granddad during the summer of '47, she'd scoot under their long front porch to play in the sand there. Despite the fun she sometimes had in the tall red brick house with the wide stairs to the second floor; the dark cellar where she wasn't allowed to go at least not by herself; the odd tall building called an outhouse which she didn't have at home with pages from catalogs for toilet paper and big holes she would almost fall into; the garage with the chicken coop under it where she helped Grandma find warm eggs the hens laid; and the narrow dirt path up to the picnic grove where everyone danced and sang and most of all ate Grandma's fine food on special days. Her place in the sand under the porch was her favorite.

Her aunts and their families usually spent Sunday afternoons after Church visiting Grandma and Granddad too so her Mom and her three sisters would sit up on the front porch above her swinging back and forth on two facing gliders and talk all afternoon while the men would play horseshoes in the back yard. Her cousins - four girls all a few years older than she was - would swing in the big tree swing her Dad built in the yard or play ball in the field beside the house.

But Grandma would stay in the kitchen cooking and baking for their big family dinner later in the day. Suzy especially enjoyed her homemade long thin noodles for her chicken soup and loved watching her cut the strands lickety-split with a long, sharp knife at the table in the room next to the kitchen; thick pieces of her Hungarian kolach bread hot out of the oven with butter oozing through them; her raised doughnuts twisted into eights which she fried in a special pan on top of the stove and then rolled in sugar. Sometimes Grandma even let her help. Suzy loved licking the extra sugar off her fingertips when they were finished.

One lazy afternoon as Suzy played in her huge sandbox under the porch, words mysteriously escaped through the cracks in the boards or flew around the ends of the wide expanse of wood above her. They seemed to drop in her lap as she scooped up handfuls of sand wetted with water she carried out from the kitchen in an old tin can to construct her buildings.

She had just started building a turret on a castle when the first words - loud, angry ones - "NO, NOT AGAIN!" rang down from above her. All she could make out after them was that someone was "on the bottle." Now that was really strange. Why would the ladies be so mad about someone being "on the bottle" again? Her baby sister Patsy still took a bottle. Could they be talking about her? But why were they so upset? After all, Patsy's still a baby. She doesn't even have any teeth yet so she can't chew anything. Suzy knew that all too well because one day just last month she had tried to feed her a piece of the orange she was eating, but her Mom got real mad at her and yanked it out of Patsy's mouth right away. Then she told Suzy she could have choked on it. So why are all the ladies on the porch so upset because her baby sister is still taking a bottle? Suzy couldn't think of even one reason why.

She continued forming the sand into a moat around her special castle. Then some minutes later from down under in her special hideaway, she overheard the words "in the family way." What could they mean? Of course, she did know what a family was. After all, she was a big "four fingers" old. A family had a dad and a mom and maybe some baby girls and boys. But what did "in the family way" mean? Her Mom and aunts seemed so upset about whatever it was. Their voices all sounded so angry. Then she heard them say something about "taking care of it." What did that mean? A baby isn't an it; it's either a girl like her or a boy like Sonny who lived next door to her. Sometimes they rode their tricycles together. Who needed care? Of what? Oh why were her Mom and aunts talking about such strange things?

Questions screwed up Suzy's rosy face. Big people just didn't make any sense. She wanted to run up on the porch, jump into her Mom's lap and ask her to explain everything to her. But she knew from her small reservoir of past experience that she wouldn't like being interrupted when she was talking to her sisters.

Imagining she was Queen Rosalind of her intricate sand castle, Suzy barely overheard the next words that filtered down to her because they came in whispers which sounded like some woman "fell off a roof." Who could that have happened to? Who got hurt? Was it someone she knew? Grandma maybe? Oh no! Is that why she isn't sitting up on the porch with Mom and the other ladies? Suzy couldn't stand not knowing. She loved her Grandma so much!

There was only one way to find out if she was OK or not. Suzy knew she just had to do it so she rubbed her sandy hands down the sides of her shorts as she crawled out from under the porch. When she reached the bottom of the stairs, she heard another whisper - a little louder one this time - that sounded like the other word for the dot at the end of a sentence, but that didn't matter or mean anything to her. She just had to find out who fell off a roof. Sobbing, she ran across the porch and climbed up into her Mom's arms.

"What's the matter, Suzy?" everyone asked. She was so afraid to hear the answers to the questions that she could barely get the words out of her mouth. "Who fell off the roof?" Before anyone could answer, she swallowed hard and continued, "Was it Grandma?" All her Mom and her sisters did when they heard her words was hold their sides laughing so hard tears rolled down their faces.

Now Suzy was really dumbfounded. She couldn't understand why all the ladies could laugh and cry at the same time especially if it was Grandma who fell off the roof! Didn't they care if she got hurt?

She had to find out for herself so she squirmed down from her Mom's lap before everyone stopped laughing and crying, ran as fast as she could across the porch, down the stairs, around the bush edged sidewalk surrounding the red brick house and onto its small back porch and then finally burst into Grandma's warm kitchen, all sweaty and out of breath.

As soon as she swung open the screen door, she squealed in relieved delight, "YOU'RE OK!" when she saw Grandma standing by the stove stirring something in a huge silver pot with her long wooden spoon. Even though Suzy felt so much better with Grandma's cushiony arms around her, her tiny heart kept pounding furiously. Then she heard Grandma ask, "What did you think happened to me, my little one?"

"I heard one of the ladies on the porch say someone fell off the roof and I thought it was you, Grandma, and I was so scared. I had to find out if you were all right. I couldn't wait for them to tell me. All they kept on doing was laughing and crying at the same time about something," Suzy breathlessly replied in one hurried sentence.

"There. There, my honey dear, just simmer down. You see your Grandma's right here and I'm perfectly fine. I haven't been anywhere near a roof and don't expect to be any time soon so why don't you just go sit on your little chair under the stairs and grind me some coffee beans?" Then she hugged her dear little granddaughter, a knowing smile dancing across her face. As Grandma intended, Suzy quickly forgot all about who fell off the roof. She felt like such a big girl helping her Grandma by getting the beans ready for everyone's coffee.

It wasn't until seven years later when "it" happened to her for the first time that Suzy really understood why her Mom and aunts laughed so hard they cried that Sunday afternoon when she was four and thought Grandma had fallen off the roof.

PART III

How can we ever separate what we
become from each of those who were
so much a part of that becoming?

Penny's Locket

On August 6, 1993 a Category 4 Tornado with a maximum wind speed of 260 mph hit about forty miles away from the city center of Williamsburg, Virginia killing four and injuring several hundred.

∽ ∾

Disorientated. Discombobulated. Disturbed. Rubble. Throbbing head. Flashes of recall. Penny? Wind. Wild. Fury. Pain. Penny? Blood. Hurt. Pain. Penny? Can't move. Head pounding. Hurt leg. Arm. Head. Storm. Fury. Penny? Where? Where am I? Where's my little Penny? No! No! Can't be gone. Not her too. Have to find her. Head. Hurt. Pain in heart. Penny?!

∽ ∾

Silas Jones slowly pulled his six foot body up off the ground. For many minutes he didn't know where he was. Then as his bloodshot brown eyes peered around the area, he groggily realized he was inside a very small completely wrecked room. The fury of the storm came back to him suddenly. There had only been enough time for him to hide in the coal cellar for protection before it struck. Now the place was in shambles around him. Shelves had tumbled on top of other shelves knocking the jars of "put up" peaches and tomatoes down. Glass was strewn over the floor covered with juice oozing from the containers. When Silas looked beyond the coal cellar, all he saw was destruction. Buildings with roofs looking as though a giant ripped them off and tossed them helter skelter on the ground. Debris of all kinds scattered across the street.

He started to walk haltingly at first and then he remembered his daughter and made his legs move faster. Where was Penny? Had her tiny two year old body been blown away by the tremendous wind? No! She was all the family he had left in the world. He couldn't lose her too. Yet, he had no idea where to even begin to look for her. He felt his forehead, realizing it was blood sticky from some kind of cut. Maybe a piece of wood or glass had hit him during the storm. The storm. Was it finally over? But where was his little Penny? Where should he look for her? Could she still be alive somewhere? He sank back to the ground just a few yards away from his coal cellar refuge. He didn't know what to do. He was at a loss for action. His mind though on low power kept prodding him, "Where's my Penny? Where's my Penny?" but all he could do was curl up in a ball and sob.

Three weeks later most of the effects of the biggest tornado in recent memory in the area had been completely cleaned up and the historic area of Williamsburg, Virginia renewed. On a bright cloudless day a trio slipped out a of a van in the visitor's parking lot - Francine, her two year old blond curly haired daughter Penny and the little girl's Aunt Laura.

"How I wish Jim could be here with us! He loves this place," Francine sighed. "Oh, I hate that Persian Gulf War! I wish he'd been able to come home by now. I really hate Penny's not knowing him."

Her sister Laura replied, "How hard too having her without him right there with you in the birthing room."

"Oh, please let's get off this subject, Sis. It's too depressing. We're here to enjoy the historic area. Come on, Penny, we're going to buy you some cookies at the bake house before we start to visit the other houses."

The little girl skipped across the brick walkway between the two women to the small bakery where they found themselves crushed in a crowd in the tiny space. Penny squealed in anticipation of her hot-out-of-the-stone-oven cookies. In the commotion of the room, the three got separated. Penny's Mom standing in line at the counter. Her sister checking out the old fashioned equipment. Penny spying a horse and buggy outside and leaving the room by herself to run along beside it all the way down the road out of sight of the bake house.

Five minutes later with a bag of goodies in her hands, Penny's Mom turned around looking for her. When she didn't see her right away, she presumed she was with her sister. In horror when the two woman connected, they realized the other one didn't have Penny in tow! They pushed their way out the door and each flew in opposite directions looking for her. Hours later, distraught and out of breath and hope, the two women sat down and cried at the Missing Persons Office.

Penny loved to run so much. She continued even after the horse and buggy stopped and pulled into a resting spot. Then she heard a man hurrying toward her calling out, "Penny, my Penny, my darling little girl, you've come back to me!"

Penny stopped suddenly and looked up at the man. "Daddy?" she asked.

The man smiled, lifting her up in her arms saying a soft prayer, "Thank you, God, for bringing my little girl back to me!" The man named Silas Jones carried the little girl in his arms all the way back to his makeshift tiny house just beyond the historic area, never noticing she was wearing jeans and a sweat shirt with flowers on it instead of the traditional long dress and bonnet of the historic area.

He didn't understand why the little girl kept asking him, "Where's Mommy?"

Each time she did, he answered softly, "Remember I told you she's gone home to God, Honey."

Penny didn't understand the man's words "home to God." She just thought he meant her Mommy left her here to go home without her. She didn't understand why, but her Daddy was with her now so he'd take good care of her. Everything was going to be all right.

One morning three years later Penny's Aunt Laura clicked on an email from her friend at the police department. A computer projection of what her niece Penny would look like today flashed up on her screen. Laura almost stopped breathing as she peered at it remembering the horrible day her niece disappeared from the bake shop in the historic part of Williamsburg. She stared at the projection of a three-year-older Penny. How terrible the years had been for all the family! Especially for her sister Francine hoping beyond hope they'd find her or some stranger would notice her off by herself somewhere and bring her to the police station. But, unfortunately, especially for Penny's Mom and for her Dad Jim finally home from an extended tour of duty in the Persian Gulf, no leads had been forthcoming.

Laura sank her rotund body down into her favorite oversized soft recliner. It was no wonder her sister didn't want to be a chaperone with her at Williamsburg today. The memories were still too painful. But she had to go; her commitment to her Girl Scout troop was a special one. Hours later as her twenty fourteen year old girls hopped off the bus, Laura told them where they were to meet in exactly two hours.

After they scurried off in various directions, Laura, their lone chaperone, sauntered down the main street alone caught up in recurring self recriminations and questions. On that fateful day three years ago, why hadn't she paid more attention to Penny while her Mom was standing in line to buy her cookies? Why didn't she hold Penny's little hand in hers the whole time? It was, after all, all her fault Penny disappeared. How could she ever make that up to her sister and brother-in-law? She was so engrossed in these thoughts she almost ran into a young girl in historic dress hurrying down the street carrying a basket of flowers. As soon as Laura looked at her, something flashed across her memory. This young girl looked very similar to Penny! No! How could that be? Could someone have kidnapped Penny here three years ago and kept her in this town all this time without the police or anyone else ever finding out about it?

Then in a millisecond another idea flashed across her mind -

DNA. The day her niece went missing, her special locket with several strands of her baby hair in it had fallen off her neck in the crush of bodies in the bakery. It was a bittersweet joy for her to retrieve it. What if in the life-is-stranger-than-fiction world, this girl really was Penny only three years older? Laura decided to take the only chance she could think of to find out.

Hurrying down the cobblestone street, she caught up with the little girl. "Hello there, Honey. You remind me of someone I used to know. In fact, you really look like her. I've been admiring your beautiful hair. Do you think you could take off your bonnet a minute and let me see all of your lovely curly hair?"

The little girl reluctantly tossed off her ruffle-edged hat as Laura surreptitiously took several strands of her hair from it and flicked them into a special pocket in her purse. "Thank you so much, young lady. I really appreciate your being so nice to me and showing me your lovely hair. Do you live near here, Honey?'

"Yes, not too far away with my Daddy."

"Oh, you do? That's so nice."

"Well, I have to go now. Daddy will be wondering what's taking me so long bringing these flowers to the house where he's working. Bye."

In the next instant Laura pulled out her cell phone and dialed the number of one of her friends at the police station. "Hi, Larry. I have a big question for you. Can you do a match test of the DNA from a very young child's hair with her hair sample from three years later?"

"Sure, Laura. Bring the strands in as soon as you can. The test should take about three weeks."

"Thanks, Larry. I'll see you first thing tomorrow morning."

Laura decided right then and there that she wouldn't tell her sister about any of this so she wouldn't get her hopes up prematurely. That night she didn't sleep well. The possibility that the little girl she met that afternoon was her niece haunted her nightmares....

A tall disheveled man was roughly grabbing a two year old girl and throwing her little body onto the back seat of his beat up car. The girl tried to scream but the man just clamped his sweaty palm over her tiny mouth....

When Laura woke the next morning, she was more than upset over the implications of her dream. Maybe she just let herself be deluded by how much the girl she talked to yesterday looked like what her niece would look like today. Maybe seeing that computerized photo did a number on her mind. Probably the DNA tests would prove there was no way the other girl could be her long lost niece who might be dead. Murdered. Lost forever. Laura chided herself for putting such hope into a random encounter that probably would lead to nothing.

Several weeks later when the detective called with the DNA results, Laura was sure her ears weren't working right. The hair strands were a match! "No, that can't be!" she nearly screamed. Penny couldn't have been in Williamsburg with a strange man for the past three years without anyone knowing. Who was the man Penny called her Daddy, the man she'd been living with? How did he keep her for all these years? What was his story?

She never verbalized any of these questions to her friend; she simply thanked him and turned off her phone. She had even bigger issues on her mind now. How was she going to tell her sister and her brother-in-law what she'd just found out? Would they believe what the DNA test proved about the little girl dressed in historic garb she met at Williamsburg? What would Jim do to the man his daughter called "Daddy" - the man who stole her away from his family? Laura knew Jim's anger all too well - his low tolerance for injustice, ineptitude and aggravation. How many times she'd witnessed what a hot head he could be if someone aggravated him or pulled his chain, particularly her.

Oh how could she tell him and Francine that she'd found their Penny? Would they think it was just another way to hurt them beyond the terrible thing she had done three years ago when she didn't keep close enough tabs on their daughter? Laura knew her sister had forgiven her the best she could because she realized she herself was partly to blame for Penny's sudden disappearance. Francine decided it was best to wait to tell anyone what she had learned.

Laura was really afraid of what Jim would do if she told him how she found and proved the girl she nearly ran into at Williamsburg was really his daughter. She knew for certain there'd be hell to pay. To the man Penny called her "Daddy" instead of him. To the police who never tracked his Penny down. To his wife who was also at least partly to blame for her disappearance and for not telling him what had happened to Penny beforehand. Even unbelievably to the President and the whole U.S. government for separating him from his family so he couldn't have been there for his wife three years ago to console her when their daughter went missing.

As Laura worried herself into a near panic, a new thought occurred to her. What if her detective friend took over from this point?

Why not let him tell the family what had happened? In fact, shouldn't he be the official spokesman anyway? From all his experience he would know how to deal with Jim. He wouldn't let him go off the deep end in anger. Relieved at this awareness Laura poured herself a cup of coffee and slipped an English muffin into the toaster. For now she wouldn't worry anymore about what to do regarding Penny. Tomorrow she'd talk to the detective in person.

Francine was feeling so depressed. It was almost the third anniversary of the day her Penny disappeared. She teared up almost every time she saw a young girl on the street, in the grocery store or even on television. She knew it was strange to feel her daughter so near when she really didn't know for sure if she was even alive. But "dead" was a possibility her mind ardently refused to accept. No matter how many more days, months and years passed without her, she "knew" as only a mother can know that her daughter was still alive somewhere.

Her current ongoing problem was Jim. Ever since he came home from the Persian Gulf War and found out Penny was gone, he'd been drunk almost every day. She didn't know how much longer the two of them could go on together with any kind of viable life. It was like they were both sunk in a dark pit and struck mute in each other's presence. It was hard enough for her when he was physically away but worse now that he was home but emotionally still worlds away. Every day he pulled himself out of bed like a wooden robot and lumbered off to work at the computer company that fortunately had kept his job for him. They didn't talk before he left in the morning. He never called her during the day and always seemed to be "away from his desk" if she called him. When he almost fell into the house at the end of the work day, all he wanted was multiple glasses of bourbon straight up. He hardly ate any dinner no matter what she made. Actually, she could have served fast food take outs every day for all he cared and that was only if he wasn't too out of it to want to eat anything.

At her wit's end about how to fix things between them, Francine thought about lining up some sessions with a marriage or a grief counselor, but she knew Jim would never agree to go to either one. He didn't trust any kind of shrink calling them all "phoney brain docs." As far as he was concerned, they were charlatans, only in the business to get big bucks and their jollies from hearing other people's problems so theirs wouldn't seem so bad in comparison. There was no way she could imagine he'd agree to talk about any of this with a stranger.

Francine stared through her kitchen window into the early morning sun. She needed to talk to someone right now, but the only person who would understand her predicament was her sister. She called her knowing Jim essentially considered her a "persona non grata" in their family and told her in no uncertain words she was not to talk to her. Nevertheless, she just had to. Still she needed to hear her sister's cool reassuring words and her kind concern. They had always sustained her in the past.

"Hi, Laura. It's Francine. What's happening your way today?"

"Everything's fine here, Sis. Are you OK?"

Francine thought she heard a hint of something odd in her sister's voice. Something strained. Something different she couldn't put her finger on which really bothered her.

"Yeah, I guess... No, I feel rather bereft today. It's almost three years since we lost Penny. Jim is drinking out of control like it's the only way he can deal with her loss and I...."

"Oh, my dear one, take heart. Things are going to be all right. I just know they are."

Again something in the tenor of Laura's voice put Francine on edge. What was it? Was she not telling her something important? "You don't sound like yourself today."

"I'm fine, Sis, but I have to leave for work now. Just remember to hold onto positive thoughts. A prayer or two would help as well. I have to go. Bye."

Francine stood staring at the receiver long after her sister hung up. She was certain something was going on with her, but what in the world could it be? Was she so angry at Jim for treating her as a non member of the family that she was backing off from her just saying trite things like pray or think positive? That just didn't sound like Laura. Ever since they were little girls born two years apart, they had shared everything even their deepest secrets. She couldn't figure what it was, but she knew something wasn't right between them for some reason. She had to find out what it was.

⌒   ⌒

Jim sank back in his swivel chair at work. The images on the screen jumped recklessly at him so he couldn't concentrate. All he wanted was at least one double bourbon straight up to get him through the rest of the day. "OK, Old Man, what are you going to do about all this crap?" he asked himself. "Your life's a mess. Your baby daughter's gone. Your wife hates you for being across the world when it happened. God damn it, what am I going to do? I can't go on like this!"

He looked up momentarily and swallowed hard as he saw his boss walking toward his desk. "Morning, Jim. How about stepping into my office for a few minutes?"

"Sure thing, Ken, I'll be right there as soon as I save what I was working on."

Several minutes later when he walked into his boss' office, Jim had a bad taste of foreboding in his mouth. So this was how the proverbial ax fell, was it? The way they let people go. He pulled up a chair and sat down ready for the worst.

"See here, Jim, my boy, I've noticed you haven't been working up to par since you got out of the service. Is there anything I can do to help?"

"It's Francine, Ken. Every day she's more depressed. I don't know how to help her."

"Losing your little girl is still a major deal between you two, then?"

"Yes, we can't seem to get beyond it. Everything reminds us of her. We just don't have a handle on what happened to our Penny."

"Well, here's the thing, Jim. I hate like hell to put this to you now but...."

Jim felt his throat go bone dry as he waited for the predictable ax to fall with his boss' next words.

"Your work has been dropping off lately, Jim. Your output. Your dedication. I'm afraid I'm going to have to put you on notice for the next month. If after that time you haven't gotten your usual self back, we're going to have to let you go. Sorry, Jim."

Knowing Ken's ultimatum was hardly a surprise, Jim still felt his insides drop to the floor when he actually heard it. How could he get himself back to his old work ways in only four weeks? Losing Penny was the worst, of course, but he continued to be plagued with nightmares all night every night. Reliving bomb attacks and having gut wrenching visions of his buddies dying in his arms and, most of all, being overcome with an abiding fear that he'd never make it home to see Francine and his baby daughter he had never met. One night he even "saw" his own bloodied body being carried out of the war zone.

When Jim would wake with a start from these nightmares, he would sigh in relief that he was home, but then he'd remember all that had happened in his absence and moan, "Oh, my baby Penny who doesn't even know me, what's happened to you, Honey? What kind of a demented person could have taken you right under the eyes of your Mother and aunt? How in the hell did those two careless women get so distracted they couldn't keep tabs on you, my little girl? To think I managed to survive all the hell of the Gulf War to come home and find out you'd disappeared! What kind of a God would let such a thing happen?"

Jim by now was slumped way down in his chair in front of his computer. This whole thing could make him lose his job on top of everything else. He wondered what he had done to deserve all this pain. With a major jolt to his entire system, all of a sudden.... *he was staring down the barrel of a gun convinced he was about to die out in the desert. His falling in love with Francine, their exciting wedding, his crying goodbye to her when she was seven months pregnant before leaving for this godforsaken place all flashed across his mind. The next thing he knew his prospective assailant was lying in a pool of his own blood. Jim never knew exactly what happened. Had he somehow shot the young kid first or had some stranger done the deed for him? There was no way he'd ever know for sure....*

He jumped when his phone rang. "God, that's probably Francine on my case again wanting me to go to some God damned shrink with her. I can't take it. I'm out of here!" he yelled to himself as he ignored the incessant rings and stumbled down the hall to the elevator. He had to have that double bourbon right away!

∽ ⌒

Laura jerked awake in the midst of another one of her recurrent nightmares.... *A huge black dog was chasing her. She ran and ran falling into a gully full of snakes and hornets....* She lay sweating, her whole body heaving. Minutes later the thought occurred to her, "What if what I'm about to tell Lieutenant Arnold opens up a pit of snakes and hornets?" She shivered but pushed that thought out of her head as she stepped into a pulsating hot shower knowing her next move was as sure as sunset - she had to tell Arnold what the DNA proved and what the little girl said about her Daddy. She dressed in her best blue suit and silver jewelry and even squeezed into a pair of navy blue patent leather heels she hadn't worn for many months. Then she drove the twenty minutes to the police station.

"Lieutenant Arnold, please."

"He's not available right now, Miss. Miss?"

"Emerson. I'll wait."

"It may be a while. He's dealing with a very sensitive case."

"I bet not more sensitive than mine," Laura noted to herself.

Almost an hour later a haggard lieutenant motioned to Laura to come into his office.

"Sorry you had to wait so long. A difficult case. They always are when little kids are involved. So what can I do for you, Ms. Emerson?"

"Please call me Laura."

"All right then. I'm Arnold."

"Well, Arnold, I don't know how to begin. What I have to tell you may be worse than what you've just been dealing with."

"So what's your story, Laura?"

"Do you recall the case of a two year old girl named Penny Hughes who disappeared three years ago in Williamsburg?"

"Sure I do. It was all over the papers and TV for months afterwards."

"Well, that was my niece, my sister's only child."

"Oh, I'm so sorry. So far we haven't had any viable leads on her case. It's very strange."

"That's why I'm here, Arnold. Several weeks ago I chaperoned a group of Girl Scouts back there at the historic area. As I was walking down the main street, I nearly ran into a girl of about five or so. She almost grabbed the breath out of my throat, Arnold! She looked almost exactly like the computer generated picture of what Penny would look like today!"

"Sorry to say, Laura, that's a rather common occurrence - a person seeing one of those projections and then thinking he saw the same person soon after."

"No, Lieutenant, there's more."

"OK, please go on, Laura."

"I remembered that we found the locket Penny was wearing the day she went missing. Apparently, the clasp broke. My sister had put several strands of her daughter's baby hair in it. So I decided on the spot that I'd do a bit of my own detective work. I befriended the little girl, told her she looked like someone I used to know. Then I commented on how beautiful her curly hair was and asked if she'd take off her bonnet. She was dressed, by the way, in an historic costume. When she did, I flicked a few of her hairs in a special pocket in my purse. When I got home, I asked a friend in forensics if he'd run a comparison DNA test on them."

"And they came back the same?"

"Yes, Arnold! And another thing - the girl said she lived with her Daddy nearby."

"So you're convinced that girl is your niece?"

"Well, doesn't all of what I told you prove that?"

"Yes and no. We can't just search Williamsburg for some little girl and her Father and grab them off the street or out of their house. We need more proof. Can Penny identify her real Dad?"

"That's the thing, Arnold, unfortunately, she can't. She wasn't even born yet when he was deployed to the Persian Gulf. If the man who took her is the one she's living with, he's the only Father she's ever known."

"Have you told her parents about any of this?"

"No, Arnold. I decided it was best not to say anything to them until we know for sure you have the man who took their daughter and, of course, especially Penny herself."

"Probably a wise decision, Laura. Here's what I'm going to do. I'll put two of my best men on the case. They'll go undercover with the updated picture of the girl and find her and the man and take it from there."

"How long do you think that will take?"

"It depends. If the man suspects something's up, he may hightail it out of town with the girl. We just don't know."

"Oh, Arnold, all I can ask for my sister and her husband and me is that you find Penny and bring her home to us."

"Well I'll be in touch as soon as I have any information. Hang tight in the meantime. Hopefully, Penny will be reunited with you and her parents soon."

"Oh how I hope and pray she will! I'll be waiting to hear from you. Goodbye, Arnold."

Laura left the police station elated yet oddly apprehensive. What if that man who took Penny does something unexpected and disappears with Penny? Will the detectives ever find them?

Silas remembered looking askance at Penny's arm last night. What had happened to the birthmark he remembered seeing when his dear Amy held her up to him right after she was born? His Amy. Why did God have to take her home? It's been so lonely and sad to live without her. From her place in Heaven, he knew she returned Penny to him after the storm. But why doesn't she have that birthmark anymore? Do children grow out of them? He didn't know.

"Daddy! Daddy!" he heard Penny call.

"What is it, dear one?" Silas asked when he walked into her

bedroom as she brushed her hair.

"As I was bringing flowers to put in the house you were working on, I met a very nice lady who told me my hair was beautiful so I took my bonnet off to show her better."

"Why did you do that, Penny?" Silas asked angrily.

Penny looked up at him surprised. He hadn't ever been mad at her before. She was very confused. "What's the matter, Daddy? Did I do something wrong?"

"Not really, Penny, but you have to understand that some people pretend to be nice and treat kids good but just want to hurt them. Remember I've always told you that the best thing to do is not to talk to strangers at all. I want you safe with me for a very long time, my Penny."

"But, Daddy, she was such a nice lady. I don't understand why you're mad."

"I'm not angry with you, Honey. It's just that I love you so much; I don't ever want anyone to hurt you, Penny."

"Oh, you're such a wonderful Daddy. I really, really love you bunches!"

"How much is that, my Penny?"

"I love you all the M and M's in every store that ever was!"

"Is that all?"

"No, I love you all the pretty dresses little girls have worn for a billion million years!"

"And then is that all?"

"Of course not, Daddy! I love you all the horses, dogs, cows, cats and every single animal that's ever lived in the whole world!"

"Then that certainly must be all."

"No, Daddy. I love you all the leaves on all the trees that ever grew in the whole wide universe! That's how much I love you, Daddy!"

Immensely pleased, Silas gave his little Penny a big hug and kiss and reluctantly sent her off to bed. Something about the woman who complimented her on her hair bothered him throughout the night.

Before she went to sleep, Penny hugged her favorite stuffed bear and told him, "Oh, Scruffy, I love my Daddy a very big lot! He takes care of me. Makes me good food to eat. Buys me nice clothes and lots of toys. He's a very, very good Daddy. I don't tell him how awful much I miss my Mommy though. I didn't understand when he told me a long time ago that she went home to God. But now that I'm a big girl, I know what that really means. I don't care because I don't believe it's true. My Mommy's not really dead. She's near here somewhere and some day she's going to come back so the three of us can be a real family again." Then Penny got down on her knees beside her bed, folded her hands and prayed, "Dear Baby Jesus, help my Mommy find Daddy and me so we all can be together again. Amen."

When the two undercover policemen, Detectives Frank Carson and Joe Farmer, arrived at the historic area in Williamsburg, they tried to blend in with the tourists. They "did" all the historic houses, little shops, and restaurants hoping they'd spot the five year old girl from the updated picture and the man she called Daddy. They imagined her in the long dress and bonnet Laura had described she was wearing the day she almost knocked her down on the main street. After three days tramping around the area playing tourists, they reluctantly reported to Lieutenant Arnold that they didn't have even one good lead. He advised them, "Tomorrow act like you are interested in buying a house near the historic area. Maybe something will turn up from that."

For the next two days Frank and Joe walked the nearby streets but didn't see any houses for sale. Then on the third day on their way back to the inn where they were staying, they noticed a building different from all the others. To call it a house would have been an exaggeration. Actually, it looked more like just a free standing makeshift room. What they didn't realize at first was that it had underground rooms as well. When the next door neighbor verified that a man and a little girl fitting Penny's description lived there, they set up a 24/7 surveillance alternating nights.

After the second night with no apparent activity in or around the very small house, the detectives decided it was time to interview additional neighbors. The fifth woman they talked to, an elderly woman named Mrs. Landrey, told them that the young girl and her Daddy who lived in that odd house had left on a vacation several days before.

"Does the man have a car, Mrs. Landrey?" Joe asked.

"No, sir. I never saw one at all. As far as I know, the two of them always walked together to the historic area and back. They both did some kind of work over there. Maybe someone at the employment office could help you on that. They would have all the information."

Another thing the undercover detectives didn't know at the time was that old Mrs. Landry felt so sorry for the little girl and her Daddy that she didn't want them to get into any trouble once she heard that these two men were asking everyone on the street all kinds of questions about them. That was why she had been hiding them in her basement for the past several days.

Actually, she had been helping Silas ever since the storm subsided three years before. She had fixed up a place for him in her basement then until he managed to get his house livable again. She was surprised when his little girl Penny turned up weeks after the storm, but by then Silas was back in his own house. She didn't ask any questions about the girl because she presumed she had been staying with relatives in the interim. What was somebody else's business was somebody else's business. She had learned that long ago when she worked in Maryland's state government offices in Annapolis.

The two detectives planned to go to the employment office the next day, but it was Sunday so the place was closed. Instead they spent the day watching crime shows on the TV in their room at the inn while devouring pepperoni and anchovy pizza from a take out restaurant in town.

That same day Mrs. Landry drove Silas and Penny to the local Greyhound station. Silas only told Penny there were going on a "Grand Adventure." He still had great concerns about her welfare. He kept wondering why her birthmark had disappeared, but it never actually occurred to him - at least not consciously - that she might not be his real daughter. He couldn't let that possibility into his brain or heart. He only knew he had to protect her no matter what.

They took seats together at the back of the bus. The tickets in

Silas' hand said "San Francisco." He didn't have a clue about what they'd do there, but they'd survive somehow. He would do whatever necessary to take care of his Penny.

※ ※

Promptly at 9 a.m. Monday morning the detectives walked into the employment office on the grounds of the historic area. The manager told them Silas Jones had been a stellar employee of the site for the past ten years during which time he suffered the death of his wife after childbirth and then the destruction of his house after the recent tornado. He and his daughter Penny welcomed visitors to the site while Silas also helped maintain the historic houses.

"Did Mr. Jones give notice he was planning to leave his position?" Joe Farmer asked the manager.

"No, Detective. Do you have information to that effect?"

"It would appear they are no longer at their place of residence. A neighbor told us Mr. Jones said he was going on a vacation."

"All I can say is that is so out of character for this man. During all the years he's worked here, he's never missed a day of work. If he has, in fact, left town suddenly as you say, something major must have precipitated that decision. He's dedicated to his only relative, his daughter Penny. He would do anything for her. My advice is to check out the Greyhound station in town. I doubt he would have enough money for two plane tickets."

The detectives thanked the manager and took his advice to go to the bus depot. From the photos they showed the clerk, they got their best lead so far. The man recognized the picture of the little girl who boarded the 8 a.m. bus with an older man he said could have been her

Father. In fact, he overheard the girl ask him, "Where are we going on our 'Grand Adventure,' Daddy?"

"So where were they off to, Sir?"

"San Francisco, would you believe? Such a long trip on a bus for a little girl."

After thanking the clerk for his information, Frank and Joe knew their next stop was to be the first place the bus let off passengers. They called Lieutenant Arnold who OK'd their plan.

Penny didn't understand why she and her Daddy left their little house so fast. It seemed like he couldn't wait to get out of town. For some reason she thought it was her fault. She remembered how angry he was the other night when she told him about the nice lady she met who asked to see her hair. Could that have something to do with why they left in such a hurry? She really couldn't say for sure, but it seemed to make sense though she couldn't figure out how. Her Daddy told her they were going on a "Grand Adventure" which started when they stayed in Mrs. Landrey's scary dark basement for a while. All she knew was her Daddy always took good care of her. He knew what he was doing even if she didn't. And besides it was really fun riding on the big bus named after a fast animal. She sat back in her seat by the window watching the trees and houses and farms and shopping centers fly by.

For himself Silas was extremely nervous though he couldn't explain why for sure. All his instincts told him someone was after his Penny so it was his job to do whatever he had to do to protect her. There was no way he was going to lose her again. After all, she was everything he had in the world. Life would be completely meaningless without her. He looked over as she stared out the window. Pure innocence is what he saw. Pure faith in him. Most important, pure love too. He was sure she'd do whatever he told her. He'd make this all a big game for her. All to keep her with him. Though he sensed her staying with him was in jeopardy for some reason, he vowed there was no way anyone was ever going to take his little girl away from him!

Laura was nervous as well. She wondered what was happening in Williamsburg. Had the detectives found Penny and the man she called her Daddy? She wanted to call Lieutenant Arnold, but he had assured her he would get in touch with her just as soon as he had any news. She knew her sister was getting more and more suspicious about how she'd been acting lately. She just couldn't let herself get into a big discussion with her for fear she'd tell her something or even hint at something she shouldn't say yet. Still, she felt so agitated inside about the whole search to find her niece and the man who kidnapped her, she had to sit on her hands until they hurt so she wouldn't call Francine.

"What's going on with Laura?" Francine kept asking herself. "Her behavior has been odd since the anniversary of my Penny's disappearance. I know something's up. I just can't imagine what it is. Maybe I'll call her again myself."

"Laura, tell me what's the matter," she begged as soon as her sister answered the phone.

"Nothing, Sis. Why do you ask?"

"I don't really know. I just sense you're not telling me

something. So what's happening, Laura?"

Laura was at a loss for words. She was well aware of the fact that her sister always knew or guessed or had some kind of extrasensory perception about what was going on with her. Had she somehow figured out that it had to concern Penny? She didn't think so.

"I don't know what to say. I guess I've just been out of sorts lately working too hard dealing with all the stresses in the emergency room. Being a nurse there isn't an easy job as you know, but there's nothing for you to be worried about or that you can do, Sis."

"But I am worried about you, Laura. Something is really bothering you and I need you to tell me what it is please!"

"Wait a minute, Francine, someone's at my door. Hey, it's that really cute painter who's doing my living room walls. Remember I told you how I wanted to fix up this old place and maybe sell it one of these days. Have to go now, Sis. Bye."

When Laura hung up on her quickly again, Francine became even more disturbed. She couldn't get a handle on what was going on with her sister. To her kitchen wall she resolved, "I'm going over there and confront her. I'll get whatever's bothering her out of her whatever way I have to. We can't go on like this any longer!"

<hr/>

As the Greyhound bus surged down the interstate, Silas sat reliving the happiest yet saddest day of his life.... He was standing next to his wife's bed as their daughter was finally born. His sweet Amy had endured a twenty-four hour labor bringing their little one into this sad world and then it was like she gave up her spirit and just like that was gone leaving Silas devastated. Penny was all he had left in his life now.

How he ever survived his wife's funeral and internment he didn't know, but he had taken care of his tiny daughter as best he could. That is until the day the tornado hit when he thought he had lost her, too, forever. Out of the blue he saw her again as she was the day he lost her and recalled it was so odd that she was wearing jeans and a shirt, not the usual historic clothes from the center. What she was wearing that day three years ago never registered with him because all that mattered was that he found her. But today on the way to a strange city far from the only home he and Penny had ever had, he was struck by this difference. It and the birthmark which seemed to have mysteriously disappeared concerned him somehow. Suddenly, he wondered, "Did they have anything to do with that woman who befriended her and asked to see her hair? No! How could they?"

As the bus roared on across country, Silas fell into a disturbed sleep.... *A stranger was grabbing his little girl out of his arms. A dark room. Lots of questions. So many he didn't understand. Then darkness. Complete and total darkness....*

Detectives Carson and Framer sped along the interstate on the tail of the Greyhound bus. Their plan was to board it at the first rest stop. Then they'd take the man named Silas Jones into custody for questioning along with the little girl named Penny he'd supposedly kidnapped. When the bus finally pulled into the parking lot, they hurried over to the door, flashed their badges to the driver and walked down the aisle looking for the man and girl, but no one matching their descriptions was on the bus! The detectives left perturbed and frustrated.

In the tiny bathroom at the back of the bus, Silas held Penny close to his chest flattening the two of them into the door. He told her they were playing a game called "Hide and Be Very Quiet." The twenty minutes that passed until he felt the bus roar out of the rest area felt like the longest day of his life. He knew the two men were looking for him and Penny. Why no one said anything about the two of them being in the rest room, let alone on the bus, mystified him.

Penny felt so scared squeezed against the door of the bathroom in Silas' arms. Something wasn't right. Why were they locked together in this tiny smelly room? She tried to squirm out of her Daddy's grip. She almost screamed, "Let me go, please, Daddy!" but he put his hand over her mouth. It was so big and wide she couldn't even get a whimper out. Now she was even more afraid. Oh how she wanted her Mommy!

Of course, the detectives had questioned the bus driver at length so they knew the man and the girl were definitely on the bus hiding in the bathroom. They decided to drive to the next stop where everyone had to exit the bus to get on another one. Lieutenant Arnold had advised them that this would be the best way to apprehend the two without any other problems.

When Silas and Penny finally nearly tumbled out of their hiding place, Alan Ringler, the bus driver, noted their exit in his rear view mirror. He knew he was harboring fugitives, but the little girl was so sweet and so attached to her Daddy and looked almost exactly like his dear granddaughter Susie, the pride and joy of his life. How could that nice man be a kidnapper as those two detectives said? He couldn't understand it. Possibly they weren't who the detectives thought they were. Maybe the men were just following a false lead. He'd watched enough crime shows on TV to know that apparently happens a lot not only in movies but even in real life.

He didn't know what to do about the man and little girl. Should he help them get away? Could he take the chance that the man really isn't a criminal? That he truly loves the girl and that she loves him in return? That they belong together? Not taken away in a police car and separated from each other. What should he do? In his mind's ear he heard his Momma lecturing him when he was a boy not much older than the little girl. "Now, Alan Honey, always follow your conscience no matter what."

～ ～

"Jim, we have to talk."

"OK, what about, Francie? The President? The weather? Your damn sister Laura?"

"As a matter of fact, it is about Laura. She's been acting really strange lately."

"So what else is new, Francine? You know what I think about her!"

"But, Jim, she's still my...."

"Sister. Yeah, yeah, I know, damn it, but she's a God awful person!"

"No, Jim!" Francine was crying now, desolate. Through her

tears she looked up at her husband pleading, "She's still my sister. I will not let you call her that!"

"Forget her, Francie! She disgusts me!" Grabbing the sports section page of the morning paper, he tore off to the bathroom and slammed the door. Francine fell down on the floor in a ball heaving. Under her breath she yelled, "Go to hell, Jimbo!"

I'm afraid. I don't know what's going to happen to us. Daddy seems so upset and jumpy. I don't understand why. Now I'm feeling the same way and so sad too. Daddy keeps looking over at me every few minutes. I just don't understand why. I wish I could tell him how much I still miss Mommy, but he seems to get very upset any time I ask about her. Oh, I'm so, so sad!

As the bus flew down the interstate, Ringler pondered his options. He could violate company policy and drop the man and little girl off at a town which wasn't a regular stop, but then how would he explain this decision to the detectives? What else could he do? Of course, he could just let the men take the two as planned and let the law sort everything out. That was the honorable way to go, but something kept getting in the way of this action. He wanted to protect the man and girl; he didn't want the police to possibly mess up their lives like what happened to him when he was eight and his Dad took him on a fun trip across country without telling anyone where they were going. Momma reported him to the police and there was hell to pay for his poor Dad. His parents were never the same together from then on. When he started eighth grade, they got divorced. For some reason he couldn't explain if asked, he sensed something like this could happen to the man and his daughter. Still, he kept hearing his Momma's voice in his head, "Alan Honey, no matter what happens in your life, always follow your conscience."

Ringer knew he had to let the detectives take the man and little girl into custody. He couldn't think of any other honorable thing to do. As he approached the stop where the detectives were to board his bus again, he swallowed hard and said a quick prayer he was doing the right thing. He knew his Momma would approve.

Jim had been sitting on the commode so long his behind hurt. He just couldn't face Francine after the way he cut down her only sister. "God damn it, they both make me so angry! I have every right to ream them out after how they let my little Penny go missing! The only way I survived the Gulf and the horror and loneliness of it all was by thinking about her. How when I got home, I'd hold her way up in the air and hear her squeal, 'Down, Daddy. Down!' Or I'd push her on a swing and she'd cry out to me, 'Higher, Daddy. Higher!' Or I'd help her take a bath, tuck her into bed at night, read her a story and kiss her goodnight. I love her so much. But, no, those two God damned women and some stranger robbed me of all of that! Robbed me of my Penny!"

Though she really didn't care any longer, Francine could hear her husband sobbing across their bedroom where she was curled up fetus style crying too. Oh how she wished Laura would talk to her – really talk to her! She always knew what was best for her to do in any situation. She'd know for sure what she should do about Jim now.

The Greyhound bus pulled into the rest stop where the two undercover detectives sat waiting in their rented car. As the big vehicle jerked to a stop, they climbed on the bus again and walked down the aisle and asked Silas and Penny to come with them. Penny was confused. At first she thought this was part of the "Grand Adventure" her Daddy had promised her, but when he kept holding onto her so tight it hurt and refused to get up and go with the two men, she realized it wasn't. All the people on the bus were staring at them. Penny got so scared she almost wet her pants. Instead, she started to cry, "Daddy, you're hurting me. Please let go!"

The detectives pulled Silas out of his seat as he reluctantly released Penny from his grasp. There was no way he ever wanted to purposely cause her any pain. In the next few minutes the three men and the little girl exited the bus as Ringler sighed deeply and hoped against hope that it was all a terrible mistake from a false lead.

At their car the detectives let Silas and Penny sit together in the back seat because the little girl kept sobbing, "Please don't take my Daddy away from me. Please! He hasn't done anything bad!" and wouldn't let go of the man's hand. Carson and Farmer watched as the man and little girl sat hugging each other.

Then Frank turned to Joe and said, "I don't know about you, but this doesn't look like any kidnapping situation to me."

"That same thought just passed through my mind too, Frank, but we have to call Arnold and tell him how all of this went down."

"Like some other deals we've been caught up in, Joe, I hate to have to follow through on this one. A lot of people are going to be affected one way or another for better or worse."

"I agree. I don't see how this little girl is going to let go of this man without an all out struggle. Let's suggest to Arnold that her parents be at the station when we arrive."

"The only problem is I understand that the little girl never knew her biological Father because he was sent to the Persian Gulf before she was born. Terrible, right?"

∽ ⁀

Of course, Silas and Penny didn't hear the detectives' conversation. They were too wrapped up in their own world in the back seat of the detectives' car to hear anything but each other's words.

"Now, now, my dearest Penny, please stop crying. Everything's going to be all right. I'll make sure of that, Honey."

"But, Daddy, why did those two men make us leave the bus and get into their car? Where are they going to take us?"

"Just on a little trip back to where we used to live."

"But why, Daddy? I don't understand."

"Well, you see, Penny, they just want to ask me some questions."

"Why couldn't they ask them on the big bus or right here?"

"It's hard to explain, Honey. I don't really understand either."

Penny gave the only man she ever knew as her Daddy a big hug and a few minutes later fell asleep in his arms as Detective Carson drove the two of them to the station. Silas was so worried he didn't know what else to do except keep holding Penny in his arms to reassure her even in her sleep that everything was going to be all right. He was deathly afraid the police would take Penny away from him for some unfathomable reason. What had he done wrong? He only loved and took care of his little daughter. What was so bad about that?

At the station Lieutenant Arnold was on the line to Laura.

"I have some good news for you for a change, Ms. Emerson."

"Remember it's Laura, Lieutenant. Please tell me."

"Well, it seems my detectives have apprehended a man named Silas Jones along with a little girl who's possibly your niece."

"How wonderful! But shouldn't you have called my sister to tell her first?"

"I thought you'd like to do that yourself, Laura."

"No, under the circumstances, Arnold, I believe it's better if you tell Penny's parents the news. To be truthful, my brother-in-law is a major hot head. If he finds out how this whole thing happened... initially because of me, and then I didn't let them know I may have found her, there's a very good chance he'll do something crazy. Maybe even violent."

"I see. Well I'll simply say we had a good lead which my men followed up on successfully."

"Arnold, you don't know how much I appreciate this. How can I ever thank you?"

"How about dinner sometime?"

"What was that?" Laura was taken aback.

The Lieutenant responded, "I'd like to take you out to dinner when this all blows over. If you don't mind..."

After a short pause, she replied, "Well, sure, why not? I would like that."

"Good! In the meantime hang tight and think positive about your niece."

～ ～

When Jim finally came out of the bathroom, he was at the lowest ebb of the three decades of his life. Nothing he had endured in the Gulf prepared him for the pain of losing his only child. He was frustrated. Angry. Extremely depressed. Most of all, he wanted to get far away from everyone, especially Francine and Laura who let his little girl be kidnapped. He was so angry at the two women! He just didn't want to go on feeling like this. He wanted out. Completely Totally OUT! He could have taken something in the bathroom, but that was what most women do to leave permanently. No, he had to do it some other way. Without further thought, he stormed out of the house, hopped into his 4 by 4 truck and sped down the street in the direction of the interstate.

～ ～

Francine stood at their bedroom window watching Jim as he left. A strange sense of foreboding raised the hair on both her arms. She shivered and hugged herself. Within less than an hour, only minutes apart, she got two phone calls. All she would remember later was they both seemed to come at the same bittersweet moment. Her husband's truck had crashed on the highway; Jim died instantly in a flash of flames streaming high into the sky and their darling daughter Penny was found safe after three years! Francine cried and laughed, laughed and cried.

There was only one other thing she could do. She called her sister.

"Laura, Laura, oh, I have such marvelous - good - great - fantastic news but also some terrible...."

She broke down sobbing as her sister responded, "What happened, Francine? Tell me!"

Francine managed to blurt through her tears, "Penny's been found but Jim's dead!" At that her sobbing escalated into a piercing wail.

"Oh, Honey, I'm so sorry to hear about Jim but so very happy about Penny! What can I do for you? Hold tight, I'll be right over."

As Francine sat waiting for her sister, her tears subsided a bit as she wondered if she should have stopped Jim from leaving the house or if he had purposely crashed his car into the retaining wall. And, joy of joys, in the next thought she wondered when she'd see Penny again. Caught in a quicksand of sadness but pulled out by joy, she prayed, "Oh dear, dear God, let poor Jim be in a better place away from the horrors of war he lived in the Gulf and the more terrible horror of finding out Penny was kidnapped. Help me and Laura live better lives from now on and help us try to forgive the man who took our Penny."

A knock at her door ended her prayer. Laura and a man in a business suit stood waiting. The two sisters rushed into each other's arms. For many minutes they stood in a deep embrace, sobbing tears of mixed sorrow and joy.

When the man coughed, the two moved apart. "Francine, this is Lieutenant Arnold. He's here to tell you more about what happened to Jim and to Penny."

The three sat down in the living room, Francine bracing herself to try to comprehend all the bittersweet details about her husband's death and her daughter's sudden "resurrection."

"I'll share the bad details first, Mrs. Hughes. Apparently, your husband was driving significantly over the speed limit on the interstate when suddenly he lost control of the car for some reason, swerved and crashed into the retaining wall. Witnesses reported seeing an animal - most likely a deer - flash across the road. Probably your husband tried to avoid hitting it and...."

"Please, Lieutenant, no more. I just hope Jim's at peace now. He hasn't been himself since he came home from the Gulf and found out Penny was missing. Oh my poor Jim! My poor, poor Jim! Now he'll never know she's been found."

"Well, to continue, Mrs. Hughes, about your daughter..."

"Oh yes, yes, please, Lieutenant. Is she OK? Where is she? When can I see her and bring her home? "

"First, she's fine. Very good, in fact. She's sustained no apparent physical or emotional problems except...."

"But how did you finally find her? What did that horrible man do to my Penny?"

"It's not that, Mrs. Hughes. As a matter of fact, that man Silas Jones has been wonderful to your daughter - very loving and protective as far as we can ascertain."

"But I don't understand. How can someone who kidnapped my daughter treat her so well?" Francine was confused. She peered at the Lieutenant, tears again welling up in her eyes and anger making her nostrils flare.

"Let's see, how can I explain this easily? As far as we know, Silas Jones erroneously believed that your daughter was his lost daughter - they both even have the same name. His Penny went missing after a tornado hit the Williamsburg vicinity only weeks before you and your sister and Penny visited. Apparently Silas found your Penny and took her in and cared for her and, most of all, loved her as his own child. She believed he was her Father since she never knew your husband. From every indication Silas and Penny are inseparable and have a bond at least as deep as an actual biological Father and his child would have."

"But, Lieutenant, what did he tell her about me? Surely, she must have asked where I was all of this time."

"From what she said, he told her you were dead. You see, his own wife had died in childbirth," Laura answered quickly.

"Wait a minute, Laura. How do you know this? You didn't have anything to do with all of this, did you, Laura?" Francine stared at her sister, her blood pressure rising.

Laura began explaining softly and slowly. "Please try to stay calm as I tell you this, Francine. Remember when I chaperoned the Girl Scout group at Williamsburg a month or so ago? Well, that day I almost ran into a little girl in an historic outfit who looked like the computer generated picture I was sent of what Penny would look like today."

"But why in the hell didn't you tell me and Jim about this?" Francine responded furiously.

"I just couldn't, Honey. I wasn't sure she actually was Penny then. I called a friend in the forensics lab to run a DNA test on her hair."

"How did you do that? I don't understand. Where did you get

her hair?"

"I knew I had Penny Sue's locket with a few strands of her baby hair in it. Remember we found it on the floor of the bakery house with the clasp broken. Well, I decided to get the little girl I almost ran into to show me her hair. When she took off her bonnet, I took a few of her hairs so I could send them to my friend to compare with Penny's baby hair in the locket."

"And they came back with the same DNA?" Francine asked.

"Yes, they did, but I still couldn't tell you until the detectives actually found the man and your Penny. I didn't want you and Jim to get your hopes up too soon so I bit my lips almost to bleeding not to tell you anything ahead of time. I'm so sorry if I hurt you, Francine, but I thought it was for the best. And I'm so very sorry Jim will never know about Penny."

Francine settled down enough at this point to add, "Under those circumstances I guess I would have done the same thing, Laura. Now, Lieutenant, I have one very important question to ask you again. When can I bring my Penny home?"

"I think for her well being, Mrs. Hughes, we have to prepare her first by explaining to her who Silas Jones really is and why he's been taking care of her for the past three years. Then we have to tell her that you are alive and anxious to see her again. What's happened to her so far, especially recently, has been overwhelming for her so we have to explain all of this to her very gently. We don't want to traumatize her anymore than she's already been or is necessary."

"So we won't tell her what happened to her real Father now? But what about that horrible man who took her? What's going to happen to him?"

"That's a real issue we face now, Mrs. Hughes. The problem is he and your daughter appear inseparable. I believe there will be untold psychological trauma for both of them if we suddenly tear them apart. Maybe you can meet and talk to Silas and try to understand him and what he's apparently unknowingly done."

"What? That sick man took my baby and kept her away from Jim, God rest his soul, and me for three long years! Surely he should be locked up and taking psychological exams."

"Time will tell, Mrs. Hughes. For now please calm down and try to decide what's best for Penny. First, she has to deal with possibly losing the only Father she's ever known and then with the trauma of realizing her Mother she was told was dead is alive. Those two announcements would be enough to shake up anyone's world. I can only imagine how an innocent five year old would react to them."

"Of course, Lieutenant, but I just don't see how I can ever look at this man called Silas let alone forgive him somehow."

"As I said, for now let's just try to figure out a plan for Penny."

Laura joined the discussion at this point, "Why don't we prepare Penny by telling her Silas thought her Mother was dead but miraculously she is back and very anxious to see her again. Do you think that could work, Francine?"

"Whatever you think is best Laura. I just want my baby back!"

The Lieutenant continued with another brainstorm, "Hold on here. Silas Jones is the only parent your little girl has really known for most of her life. I don't think we want to risk upsetting her more than she has already been by indefinitely separating her from Silas. Do you think she'd recognize your voice if she heard it, Mrs. Hughes?"

"I suppose she might. If she does, then I could tell her how things happened and then go into the room where she is. Is that what you have in mind, Lieutenant?"

"By the way, long before now we should have been on a first name basis. I'm Arnold. You're Francine, right?"

"So, Arnold, do you think what I said will work?"

"We'll try, Francine. What's your take on all of this, Laura?"

"Well, another possibility is I could go into the room first. Hopefully, Penny will recognize me from the day we met recently when I asked to see her beautiful hair. Then I could tell her I have a big surprise for her - that her Mommy isn't really dead but is right outside the door to take her home."

"I like that better than her hearing my disembodied voice, Laura. You can always come up with such great ideas. Let's do it. Oh, I'm so anxious to hold my baby in my arms again!"

"One more thing, Francine. Because of how all of this went down and your daughter's fear she'll be separated from Silas, she may not be ready to accept you so quickly and go home with you leaving him behind. What do you want to do if that happens?"

"Let's decide that if the situation warrants it, Arnold?"

"Yes, we can do that, but the two of you, especially you, Francine, need to be prepared to for a less than 100% welcome. This little girl seems extremely confused. She doesn't fully understand what's been happening especially since she and Silas left Williamsburg so suddenly. Each of us has to be careful about what we say to her and be very easy on her."

Francine shook her head in agreement and asked, "What will happen to that man Silas Jones who took her?"

"He'll have a psychiatric evaluation. Most likely they'll put him in the old mental hospital near the interstate."

"They won't release him until he gets better, will they?" Francine questioned with worry in her voice.

"I can't say really. He's a special person whose spirit and brain have been impaired from the effects of the tornado three years ago so he's been quite traumatized too. It appears that finding Penny was what saved him from going off the deep end completely. It would appear she gave him renewed strength to go on with his life after the storm."

Now it was Laura's turn again to put her two cents' worth into the discussion. "If that's all true, Arnold, maybe we should arrange some way the two of them can stay in contact. We could perhaps even visit Silas in the institution eventually. What do you think, Francine?'

"I don't know, Laura. Maybe after I meet Silas and talk to Penny and see the situation for myself, I'll agree with you. Or not. I don't know. Right now I just have to see my baby. Can't I please do that now, Arnold?"

"Sure, Francine. But just for the record I have to repeat that this probably won't be easy for either of you and certainly not for her. You both need to try to stay cool and calm no matter what."

In the meantime at the police station a social worker was trying to talk to Penny to reassure and console her.

"Where's my Daddy?"

"He's busy now, Honey. Some men are talking to him."

"Why? We were going on a 'Grand Adventure' and those men in black suits took us here. When can I be with my Daddy again? I miss him so much."

"Why don't you have some milk and chocolate chip cookies while you wait for him? Everything will be all right, Honey."

"That's what my Daddy tells me."

Penny sipped the cold milk and munched on the cookies trying to be brave like her Daddy would want her to be.

As soon as Francine and Laura walked into the station, they felt increased trepidation and concern. Laura about how she would react to meeting the man who took her niece. Francine about how her baby girl would react when she realized she was really alive. Would she jump up and hug and kiss her or would she refuse to acknowledge her and cry for Silas, the only Father she'd ever known? Francine had to force herself to be calm and loving and understanding no matter what happened. Penny was a little girl not yet six years old who probably couldn't understand much of this. She had to be patient that she'd make it through this. She had to be willing to wait for her daughter to accept and love her again.

As the three approached the room where Penny sat talking to the social worker and enjoying her snack, Francine stopped everyone in their tracks and announced to the Lieutenant, "I have to talk to Silas Jones before I see Penny. I have to try to understand who he is and how all of this happened. Most of all, I have to try to understand how my Penny has come to love him so much as her real Father."

"OK, Francine. I can arrange that."

Lieutenant Arnold knocked on the door of the room where Detective Farmer was questioning Silas. He motioned the Detective to come out in the hall to talk.

"Farmer, Mrs. Hughes would like to talk to Jones before she reunites with her daughter."

"Sounds like a plan, Lieutenant. Hopefully, it'll go well. We'll keep watch and listen from the next room."

What struck Francine immediately about Silas was his calm and almost boy-like demeanor. He looked up at her with clear eyes and a serene face. Detective Farmer did not tell him in advance who he'd be talking to. He deemed it best if she tell him herself when the time was right and he was ready to hear and comprehend her announcement. Francine simply began with, "Hello, Silas. My name's Francine. I understand you've been taking care of a little girl named Penny."

"Yes, that's right. My daughter. I love her so much. Do you know where they've taken her? I miss her."

"I'm sure she misses you too, Silas. I have something that you need to hear and understand. You see, Silas, the little girl you've been calling your daughter is actually my little girl."

"What? How can you come in here and tell me that? She is my Penny. I saw her being born right before my dear Amy died. No, you're wrong. That can't be!" At that Silas punched his fist several times on the table and then became silent.

Francine refused to just leave. "Please try to understand what I'm telling you, Silas. A DNA test from Penny's hair matched my

Penny's hair in a locket she lost at Williamsburg three years ago. Apparently you found her walking down the street weeks after the big storm, thought she was your daughter Penny and took her."

"No! No! This isn't true. I told you I saw her being born just before my wife left this earth. You can't be her Mother and she can't be your daughter! I'm her Father. Her Mother's dead. I don't care about some test!"

Silas was now on the verge of a breakdown. Different clothes and a disappearing birthmark and a story about a stranger admiring Penny's hair came back to his memory in a rush, but he pushed them all away just as fast as they came. "No, she can't be yours! She's mine. Only mine!"

Francine was stymied. She didn't know how else to convince this poor man that Penny was her daughter. She felt his pain as she tried to imagine being in his shoes.

"Silas, you must be overwhelmed by what I've just told you. A very special scientific test proved that the little girl you've been so nicely taking care of is not really your daughter. You saw some other baby girl being born before your wife died. That little girl, your real daughter, died in the tornado three years ago."

"No, I said no! No! She's mine!"

When Francine left the room abruptly, Silas' head dropped down on the table.

～ ⁄．

The Lieutenant and his two detectives on the case had heard and seen what Francine had just experienced with Silas. They left the adjourning room as she walked out into the hall. "Mrs. Hughes, please don't be discouraged. From what we can ascertain, Silas is a man who just can't comprehend certain things, DNA testing for one. We'll have to find some other way to reach him."

"What about Penny? Maybe she can convince him who I am."

"Perhaps, but Penny may not recognize you. As I've said, even if she does, she may be torn between the man Silas she's known as her Father and you she barely remembers, if at all."

"Oh, Arnold, what am I going to do?"

"There's only one thing now. Come with me to see your daughter."

"But what if she doesn't remember me? What then?"

"Hopefully, she will, Francine. If not now, eventually."

"Then I guess I'm as ready as can be. Do you want to go in first, Laura, to prepare her for a big surprise as you suggested earlier?"

"Sure, Francine."

Laura slowly opened the door. The social worker got up as she did and slipped out of the room.

"Hello. Do I know you?" Penny asked right away.

"Yes, you do, Honey. We talked a while ago at Williamsburg and you took off your hat and showed me your pretty hair. Remember?"

"Yeah, I told my Daddy what a nice lady you were."

"Well, before that, Honey, do you remember going there in a big van when you were real little?"

Penny didn't answer but seemed attentive.

"We went to the bakery house and then you disappeared. Do you remember the two ladies you were with that day, Penny?"

"I don't know."

"Well I was one of them, Honey. I'm your Aunt Laura. Do you think you might remember me?"

"Were you with my Mommy?"

"Yes, she was there too, Penny."

"But she is dead."

"No, Honey, Silas told you another woman was dead. He was talking about the Mother of his daughter, not your Mother. Please listen to me very carefully, Honey. Mr. Silas is very confused. He thought you were his daughter because his head got messed up in the big storm that killed his real daughter. He wanted her to be alive so much that when he saw you, he believed you were his daughter."

"But he is my Daddy!"

"I'm going to tell you something that you have to try very, very hard to understand. A special test proved for sure that you are not Silas' daughter."

"No!"

"Silas is a nice man who took care of you since that day your Mommy and I lost you in Williamsburg. Now we're here to take you home with us."

"But what about my Daddy?"

"He has to stay here for a while. But your Mommy's waiting right outside. Do you want to see her now?" A long moment of silence passed before Penny looked up at Laura.

"Yeah," Penny mumbled, confused and unsure.

Laura cracked open the door and motioned for her sister to come into the room as she stepped out. Cautiously, Francine walked in smiling at Penny. She was trying hard not to pick her up and hug her for all the days, months and years she couldn't.

"Hello, Penny. How are you?"

"I'm fine," the little girl responded slowly.

"Do you know who I am, Honey?" Francine's eyes began to well up; she had dreamt of this moment more nights than she could count.

"No."

"Did your Aunt Laura tell you about Silas' mistake?"

Penny looked away, detached.

"Did she tell you that your real Mommy hasn't gone to Heaven? That she isn't dead?"

"Yeah."

"Did she say she's here?"

"Uh huh," and she shook her head yes.

"Well, would you like to see her again, Penny?"

"Yeah."

"Well, here I am, Honey," as her voice got very soft, the tears dripping onto the floor. "It's Mommy. Do you remember me?"

Penny shook her head. She wanted to remember her Mommy, but she was afraid she'd hurt her Daddy somehow if she did. She didn't know what to do. With little tears flowing onto her shirt, she looked up at Francine.

"Oh, Honey, that man Silas..."

"You mean my Daddy."

"Oh, Honey... I have something else to tell you now. Since you're not Silas' daughter, he can't be your Daddy. Your real Daddy died yesterday in a car accident, Penny."

"No, Mommy. He's alive! I want to see him!"

"Oh, my dearest Penny," Francine knelt down next to Penny
and hugged her. "I missed you so much. I'm so sorry your real Daddy
never got to know you. He had to be very far away when you were
little."

"Mommy!?"

The woman and the little girl sat hugging each other for a long
time. Then Penny asked her again, "But what about my Daddy? What's
going to happen to my Daddy?"

"Honey, I know he seems like your Daddy but..."

"No, Mommy, he is my Daddy! Where is he? I need him. He is
my Daddy! Daddy! Daddy!" Penny began yelling for her Father, her
Father that wasn't really her Father. Yelling for a Father that was dead.
For a Father that didn't exist except in the confused mind of a child.

"Oh, Honey, it'll be fine. I promise. He has to stay here to talk
to the detectives. When they're finished, then we'll decide what to do."

Francine squeezed her daughter's tiny hand in hers as they left
the room. Laura, Arnold and the two detectives smiled as they walked
down the hall together.

Just as they passed by the room where he was sitting, Silas
called out to Penny, "Where are you going, my Penny? Penny! Penny!"

"Silas," Francine turned and answered, "I'm taking my
daughter home."

"What have I done? Don't take my daughter! Oh, Penny, come
back to your Daddy."

"I can't right now, Daddy. I have to go home with Mommy."

"But she's in Heaven, Penny."

Penny started crying again, being torn between both persons.

"Penny!" Silas continued to scream.

Francine couldn't stand it anymore and told Silas, "You really wanted this little girl to be yours because your real Penny died in the tornado years ago. Don't you remember that they found her near your house? Apparently, her little body was taken away by the horrible winds and later landed and became covered with debris."

"No! My Penny isn't dead. She's here. She's not with my Amy in Heaven. I can't be left all alone!"

"But I'm still here, Daddy," Penny responded grabbing Silas' big hands in hers and then hugging him. Francine gently pulled Penny away and they left the station.

Silas fell to the floor distraught to the tips of his toes.

Within a week of Jim's burial, Francine made the hardest decision of her life. For her daughter's sake she agreed to chaperone Penny on her visits with Silas at the institution where he now lived.

Within several months, they began to visit him less and less as Penny grew to accept that he was not her real Daddy. One day when the two sisters went shopping with Penny at the local flea market, it started to rain hard. Laura ran under the large tent where they served food. When Francine ran up to her, drenched and cold, they realized that Penny was not with either of them....

The Moon Lite Motel

What a shock it was to Tina's system to see the place again after so many years as she drove by it on the way home from a reunion with her girlfriend Paula. To describe the building as dilapidated would be a blatant understatement. Every area where a room used to be was barely hanging together by a few boards. The doors had been apparently been torn off so each room looked like a dark hollow space. The errant weeds and grass tried to cover up the depressing scene to no avail. The whole area reminded her of a old woman, wrinkled and weary, who hadn't paid any attention to her personal appearance for ages.

Tina wondered how many years it had it been since she stayed here? Thirty? Forty? Then suddenly the events of that night all came back to her in a rush....

～ ～

My Senior Prom May 1976. Marty Henderson my date. A night I could never forget. Wearing a long black silk backless gown everyone said made me look so sophisticated and much older than my barely seventeen years. Feeling so beautiful and sure of myself. Marty, arriving at my parents' house, looking so handsome in his black tux with a red plaid cummerbund, whistling at me and squeezing my hand. My Dad taking photo after photo of the two of us.

I was elated! Flying high in the glory of the evening ahead of us as we sped off to the local country club in Marty's father's sleek black Mustang convertible. Singing Beatles songs on the way. Feeling so young and free and happy!

The Prom itself proved uneventful and less than exciting despite all our anticipation in advance. Yes, we danced to the four person rock band and even did some involved line dances with our friends. But Marty and I just wanted to be alone. To have the rest of the night just to ourselves.

We had planned our own private "After Prom Party" for weeks. We'd leave the Prom early. Change into older looking regular clothes we had "borrowed" from our parents' closets. Then check into the Moon Lite Motel in the next town as newlyweds Mimi and Art Garland. How soon we learned that Life throws fast pitches out of the ballpark despite our best laid plans!

First, we didn't know ahead of time that Marty's sister's best girlfriend Cindy had just started working the front desk of the motel. She checked us in smirking and mumbling under her breath what sounded like, "Newlyweds!?" I don't think she actually recognized us, but she surely saw through our "disguises."

When we opened the door to the even then shabby room, I felt the mustiness almost choke me. I noticed the beige bedspread was stained in several places and ripped down the right side. The discolored lamp shade by the bed had what looked like a cigarette hole in it. The whole place made me feel dirty and depressed.

Marty was pulling off my jacket before I could get my breath. All of a sudden despite our careful plan for this Night of Nights, which was to be The First for both of us, I didn't want anything to happen. My body went limp as I became disgusted with myself and with Marty, but he didn't seem to notice my upset at all. As he started to unbutton my Mother's blue shirt, he was breathing heavily. Then he started to caress me.

At that point it was as though a loud alarm sounded in my panicked brain. I really didn't want to do this. I didn't want my - our - first time to be in a place like this and based on a lie that the busybody Cindy at the desk knew we were telling. I tried to pull away from Marty. He looked up at me in disbelief.

"What's wrong, Hon?"

"It's just...."

"Look, this is the special night we both planned. Let's enjoy ourselves, Mrs. Garland!"

He laughed at his joke staring into my eyes which were bubbling with tears. I didn't know what to answer. How to tell him it was all off. That I really didn't want to do anything.

Unfortunately, he misinterpreted my reticence to answer as a tacit approval to continue. Suddenly, he kissed me hard with a passion which was new to me. I started to perspire, fear surging inside me. He wouldn't force me to go through with this, would he? No, not Marty. Not the guy I've known since first grade. Not the guy who held my hand on our first roller coaster ride. No, not my Marty! Still I could feel his hardness now against my body though my skirt and his slacks and I knew I had to stop him!

"Marty, please, I'm not ready. Wait!"

"But, Tina...."

"I have to...."

"Oh, of course. Sure, sure. Go to the john. I'll be out here waiting."

I stumbled the few feet into the tiny bathroom where I threw up all the hors d'oeuvres I ate at the Prom into the rust edged toilet bowl. Then I wiped my mouth, rinsed it and sat down on the commode shaking with ambivalence about what to do.

Marty really wanted to do "it" now. But I didn't! How was I going to get out of it? What could I do? I looked at the window in the bathroom but it was too small a square. I knew I'd get stuck if I tried climb out of it. And even if I could and did, what would I do then? Ask that snooty Cindy to call my parents to come and pick me up? No way!

I had to think of something else. A period. My period. It wasn't due for two weeks. Could I pretend it had come early? I'd need some blood. I'd have to cut myself somewhere Marty wouldn't notice. I decided I'd cut the little finger on my right hand, then wrap it up in toilet paper after first, of course, wiping some of the blood around the inside of my legs.

Out in the bedroom Marty was getting impatient waiting. "Hey, Tina. Are you OK?"

"Yeah, Marty. I'll be out in a few more minutes. I have to tell you something."

When I walked back into the bedroom a few minutes later, I know my face was ashen. I had cut my pinky too deeply with the jagged piece of the glass I broke against the bathroom sink. The trouble was I couldn't stop the surge of blood. As soon as he saw me, Marty knew I was not all right.

"Come over here and sit down, Tina. You don't look so good."

"Oh, Marty. It's just that my period started. I'm sorry."

Tears dropped down my face. My finger was throbbing with pain now and the blood was oozing through the toilet paper I had wrapped around it. The next thing I knew I was falling, falling....

Tina turned into a gas station trembling so much as she relived that night after the Prom that she couldn't keep driving. Deciding a quick jolt of caffeine would help, she bought a large coffee and a cinnamon bun. She hadn't eaten breakfast before she left her girlfriend's house this morning. They enjoyed a late dinner last night reminiscing about the old days. A few quick gulps and bites relaxed her enough to reluctantly remember what happened next so many years ago....

Marty was quite solicitous. But he was no dummy. He put two and two together when I fainted and he saw my wrapped up finger dripping blood and called 911. The next thing I knew I woke up in a bed in the Emergency Room of the local hospital with my parents towering over me and Marty sulking in the corner. My Mom and Dad, of course, blamed him for what had happened though I never told them the whole story.

Over that summer Marty and I drifted more and more apart. I never told him what really happened either. Going off to colleges on either coast was the death knell of our friendship. Looking back, I realized Marty was never meant to be "My First." Who was is another story....

∽ ∾

Tina was now an hour away from the site of the dilapidated Moon Lite Motel. There was no way she could ever forget what had almost happened as well as what actually did happen there that night so many years ago after her Senior Prom.

She called home at the next rest stop. Her husband Richard, Marty's best friend who attended Stanford at the same time she did, was happy to hear from her and anxious for her to get home. As she clicked off her cell phone, she wondered if Marty had ever told him about the night four decades ago that she had just relived. Probably not was her guess.

Joey and the Mass

Roz really needed to get away. Her life was so hectic with four teenage girls at home, not to mention the hundreds she attempted to teach in her five high school French classes every day.

How happy she was to find out about the hermitage on the lake which had a canoe for her use as a wonderful added attraction! Down the hill from the Franciscan Friary that owned it, across the parking lot to the gate to the driveway for fishermen to the lake, the first right turn after the concrete parking area, then a walk down about a city block through the woods. There it stood tucked away among the tulip trees a few feet from the edge of the lake. What a lovely escape place for a week of solitude and peace!

In the middle of her first night there, Roz was awakened by strange sounds. Caught between the world of waking and sleeping, she sat up in bed trying to identify what she had heard. It sounded like a combination rutting/fighting/squealing noise. Being a city dweller, the best explanation she could imagine was that several deer or raccoons or maybe even the legendary bobcat someone had told her about had set up battle stations right outside her little one room with toilet on the lake. No way was she venturing out on the porch or even opening the sliding glass doors, for that matter, to find out for sure. Eventually, she fell back into an uneasy sleep.

The next evening Lisa, a graphic artist from the art center up the hill, came to see the place. As they sat talking on the porch, male voices startled them. Apparently, the two men who walked up to the porch had disregarded the sign on the path that said, "Hermitage. Bypass please."

In minutes Roz noticed that there was something strange about the taller of the two. He seemed disoriented, out of sync with things, odd in some not exactly describable way. When he started to ask pointed questions about the place, the two women were quite understandably reluctant to answer.

"You ladies live here?"

"Why yes. Yes, we do." (We didn't want to let them know that actually only one of us was staying there.)

"So what do you two do here?"

"Well it's a retreat place. Didn't you see the hermitage sign up on the path?"

"Oh yeah," the other man chimed in. "We saw that, right, Joey? But, hell, we'd never heard of any, what did you call this, hermitage? So we kept on walking down here."

By this point the two women were feeling even more uneasy

about divulging any more information. They only wanted the two men to leave. But how to suggest that without upsetting them to some kind of uncalled for reaction? And anyway maybe they were overreacting. Too much city living had made them very suspicious of strangers.

"Well, you see this is a place to pray so if you two would please..."

"Right, we get you. We'll be on our way back up the hill now. Bye, ladies."

At that they disappeared up the path as quickly as they had appeared a few minutes before.

"So what did you think about them?" Lisa asked.

"For one thing that tall one seemed strange."

"Yeah, he really did."

"But maybe they were just being curious."

"But, Roz, the problem is you're going to be down here all by yourself tonight. What if they come back?"

"Don't worry about me, Lisa. You just get back to the center. I'll be fine."

Lisa reluctantly walked back up the path, leaving Roz by herself again. Even though she still did feel just a bit apprehensive, she resolved that she wasn't going to let her imagination get the best of her. She made herself a cup of tea and sat on the porch until it got too dark to see anything across the lake.

Again she was jolted awake in the middle of the night only this time to smile in awe as she looked up to see the full moon shining through one of the three pseudo loft windows in the front of the hermitage. How utterly beautiful! She stayed awake for a long time staring up at the sky and listening to the lilting songs of the tree frogs.

The next morning she jumped out of bed at 7 to go out in the canoe. After covering up the house keys and the canoe's lock key in the grass under one of the trees in front of the hermitage, she carefully maneuvered herself into the boat and paddled her way out onto the lake. She loved mornings like this all by herself! She felt like an Indian living hundreds of years ago paddling on the lake in early morning possibly rowing to the other side to find food for the day.

A half hour later when Roz came back to the little cove where she chained the canoe to the stilts of the hermitage, she felt a wave of uneasiness wash over her like the water covering the fish in the lake. The keys seemed to be in a different place or was she just imagining they were? Maybe she just forgot where she left them in her hurry to get out on the lake earlier.

Carrying the paddle, she put the key in the lock to open the door. "That's strange," she thought, still without registering any real alarm. "This door actually opened easily today." Since she usually had trouble with keys and locks, she was relieved not to have further hassle to get into her small hermitage to enjoy a fine week of solitude and peace.

As she stepped inside, she noted everything seemed to be in place - her laptop on the table, her assorted bags around the room. "You really better get hold of yourself if you're going to stay here for a week," she warned herself, trying to still her growing apprehension she didn't quite understand. Almost as soon as that resolve passed her mind, she thought she heard something. A noise she couldn't identify for sure which seemed to come from the bathroom, just a very small room with a commode. (Having no shower was the major disadvantage of the place especially with the summer's heat and humidity. She had to walk up the hill to one of the dorm buildings to bathe. The problem would be by the time she walked back down the hill to the hermitage, she would be so sweaty she'd need to shower again.)

Roz stepped over to the bathroom to put the paddles behind the door and hang the key on the left wall. As she did she noticed that the door was closed although she always left it open. She didn't like being all cooped up in such a small space for even the few minutes it took for her to take care of business. She tried to turn the knob, but it wouldn't give. It was like someone was holding it from inside the way she and her sister had done many years ago when they were kids and tried to "get" each other. As a matter of fact, that's just what it felt like now. Someone was holding on to that door from the inside! Someone was in that tiny room!

Without hesitation Roz picked up the phone on the wall nearby, but like the night before when she had tried to reach her husband at home a thousand miles away, she couldn't get an outside line. In fact, she couldn't even get an inside call through to the priest in charge of the hermitage.

She felt sweat rolling through her eyes and down the crook of her back. Before she could even think about what do next, she heard the commode flush. Then to her complete amazement the strange man named Joey from the night before stepped out of the bathroom!

"What are you doing here? What do you want?" she asked the intruder as calmly as she could under the circumstances.

"Now don't you fret, my Little Lady. I'm going to take mighty good care of you. Just go over there and sit down on the bed."

Before Roz could refuse, the man flashed a knife across her line of vision. Without hesitation she did as he said.

"You seem to be one right smart person. Good. Good for you!"

"What do you want? My friends up at the monastery and in the art center will be wondering about me."

"Don't you worry. I've taken care of all that for you in advance. I typed up a note all by myself telling them you want to stay down here by yourself for a while and don't want to talk to anyone. Not even that friend who lied and said she was staying here with you. What was it you said last night, you wanted to be alone right here in this place to pray? Now, listen here, you're going to do just that. You, my dear Little Lady, are going to say one hell of a lot of prayers here with me. "

"But... but I don't understand. Why do you want me to pray with you? There are lots of priests and brothers up at the Church who'd be glad to pray with you. Mass is at 11:45. You can go with me."

"Didn't you hear me? You're not going anywhere! You already left them a message saying that."

Joey flashed the shiny knife in her face again as he sat down beside Roz on the bed. She tried to stand up, but he just pushed her back down in an off hand, yet oddly gentle, she thought, kind of shove.

"Listen here, I said you're going to pray with me and I mean it. So now let's get started."

"What kind of prayers do you want to say?"

"The Our Father would be a very good one to start with."

As the two recited the words, all Roz could think about was the way her four daughters had always so willingly prayed the same prayer with her when she had a special intention. She hoped maybe somehow they knew how much she really needed their prayers now.

Suddenly, the man grabbed her hand and squeezed it. "That's how it's done when you're finished saying it in Church, isn't it?"

"Yes, some people do that kind of as a finishing touch."

"Yeah, I remember that from one time last year. This real old lady sitting beside me did that. It felt real good. You do it now. Come on, let's say that Our Father prayer again and then you squeeze my hand at the end."

Roz did what the man told her, deciding if she could humor him maybe she could get away somehow by tricking him without his realizing it.

"For thine is the glory and the power for ever and ever. Amen."

"Now, now, squeeze my hand!"

Roz did as he asked only he wouldn't let go. She squirmed trying to pull away, but he was so much stronger than she was. For a few minutes she didn't know what she or he would do next.

Finally, his grasp slackened and he let her hand drop as he jumped up and walked over to the sliding door.

"You see those lily pods out there - they make nice coverings. They cover up stuff real good."

She couldn't imagine what he had on his mind. But she tried to get him thinking about something else.

"You know they only bloom in the morning."

"Well, that's right nice, I'd say. Them's pretty flowers."

He turned around and faced her. She could sense that the next step of his plan, whatever that might be, was about to happen.

"Stand up. I SAID STAND UP! NOW!"

Roz hadn't eaten breakfast before she went out on the lake so now she felt sick to her stomach. As she got up, a wave of nausea hit her. She steadied herself before speaking again.

"You never told me how you got in here and why."

The intruder roared a big belly laugh and then announced, "Easy. I watched you leaving to go out on that boat. Lovely Lady, you're going to be my salvation, you hear. You're going to be my salvation. Yes, you are. Indeed you are!"

"What do you mean - your salvation?"

"All in good time. You've heard that line, haven't you? All in God's good time. Now just go over there and make us some coffee. I noticed you have all the fixings for meals here. Looks like you and me could live in this place for some time."

"But, Joey, that's your name, isn't it?"

He shook his head looking into her eyes with a steely stare.

"How'd you know that? Oh yeah, yesterday when we first met. So what's your problem? Don't you want to get us some breakfast? I'm real hungry. You must be too. Going out so early in that canoe all around the lake. Remember I said I watched you."

"It's just that I have to call my husband. He's expecting to hear from me today... this morning."

"Well, you're not calling him or nobody else and that's that! No calls. No going nowhere. Just you and me. Just you and me that's all!"

Trying to appear very calm, Roz decided she'd start the coffee to clear her mind to decide how to deal with this man holding her prisoner for his "salvation," whatever that meant. She had to figure out a plan to get away from him.

She noticed now that Joey was leafing through the big Bible on the desk, turning the pages with the edge of his knife. He started humming the tune to the Bible school song her Protestant childhood girlfriend used to sing, "Yes, Jesus loves me. Yes, Jesus loves me. Yes, Jesus loves me. The Bible tells me so."

She wondered what her friend Juliana she'd known since she was three would do in this situation. Actually she was quite sure she would willingly sit down and pray all day with this man. Juliana was always so much holier and more devout than she ever was.

When she handed Joey his mug of coffee, he smiled and said, "Thank you, Lovely Lady. Right kind of you. Now pull over that lawn chair in the corner and come and sit down beside me."

"But don't you want anything to eat?"

"Nope. I'm not too hungry right now."

Reluctantly, Roz did what he asked. She noticed his knife was now on the edge of the desk. If she reached for it....

Joey must have read her mind because he yelled, "No fancy hero stuff, no siree! Just keep your eyes and your hands to yourself, Little Lady."

For a few minutes the two sat drinking their coffee in silence. Then abruptly, Joey's voice broke the calm. "All right, all right, here's the deal. You are going to help me get away from that place where my brother put me. I hate it there! You are going to pray here all day with me and then you are going to take me in your car up by that path past that hermitage sign. Then you are going to drive me and you into the sunset. Just like the end of those movies on TV."

"But won't everyone be worried about you, Joey? Won't that man who was with you last night wonder where you are?"

"No, Ted can't worry 'bout no one. Not anymore."

"What do you mean? What happened to him, Joey?"

"I took care of him. Don't you worry 'bout him."

"But... tell me what you did."

"No. You're talking too much. We need to start praying. Come on now. Get down on your knees beside me. Now I lay me down to sleep. I pray the Lord my soul to keep. If I should die before I wake, I pray the Lord my soul to take... That's a nice prayer, ain't it?"

"Yes, Joey. It's a nice prayer. But it's for bedtime and we're both awake. It's not night now."

"But it will be soon. We have to get ready. We need to say lots more prayers together."

"Which one do you want to say now?"

"I'll start and when I stop you fill in."

"Yes, yes, I will."

"Lovely Lady, dressed in blue, teach me how to pray. Jesus was just your little boy and you know the way... Your turn now."

"Hail Mary full of grace, the Lord...."

"No, that's not right. That's not the rest of it. Keep on with the rest!"

"But, Joey, I don't remember it."

"Well, you better! That's all I have to say. You better if you know what's good for you!" he announced, brandishing his knife once more in front of her face.

"I'm sorry but I really can't remember the rest of the words."

"I'll help you. They go something like... No! You have to say them. It's your turn!"

"Lovely Lady, dressed in blue, teach me how to pray."

"Wait, you're trying to fool me. They's just the same words I just prayed. Get up!"

He pulled her up from her kneeling position by the side of the bed. "You make me some toast now. I'm too hungry to pray anymore. Maybe later."

Relieved to get up, Roz walked over to the refrigerator and pulled out a loaf of bread and some butter and jam. While the bread was in the toaster, she tried to think about what to do. If only the phone worked, she could call 911, but aside from the fact that he had a knife, Joey really didn't seem like a major threat. She had to convince him to go up the hill with her to Mass. Then she'd have a better chance to get away from him and get some help. When she handed him a plate with two pieces of toast on it, he appeared to be reading the Book of Job if she wasn't mistaken. At least he had turned to one of the pages in that part of the Old Testament.

He looked up at Roz as he noted, "That poor son of a b really had it bad, eh? Makes me almost cry for him. I know what he's going through. Bad breaks. Everything going wrong. God giving up on him."

"No, Joey, God didn't give up on him. That's not how the story ends. God loved him a lot and was only testing him. In the end he rewards him with lots of land and riches."

"Well, that ain't the way he's treated Joey. No, he didn't give him no good stuff. He only got him locked away with no buddies and no nice car and no nice clothes and no nice ladies like you. That God up there, he don't like Joey. No, he don't like Joey one little bit. No, not at all!"

"Please don't get angry. Why don't you eat your toast? Maybe you'll feel better then."

"Whatever you say, Lovely Lady dressed in blue. Whatever you say."

Joey sat munching on his toast as Roz watched an early morning fisherman across the lake. Would there be any way she could get his attention?

Joey grabbed her arm. He seemed to be reading her mind again.

"No, there's no use trying to get him to help you. He's my lookout."

"You wouldn't just be saying that, would you, Joey?"

"No, I wouldn't fool you. He really is. That there is Frank."

Not convinced that he might be the other man from last night, Roz took a deep breath and looked over at Joey. Now he was reading the journal entries other retreatants had written in the in the hermitage book. When he came to hers, he stopped and said, "Lookie here. This is yours, right? Roz Donald, glad to meet you." He held out his hand.

Roz reluctantly shook it as she asked, "How did you find out my name?"

"Don't worry your pretty blond head none. I have ways."

"OK, I guess it doesn't matter now anyway."

"You got that right."

"So, Joey, please come to Mass with me in the big church. You'll like it."

"No, I just want to stay and pray here with you, Roz."

"But Joey..."

"Anyway why would I have to go up there to pray? God's everywhere, isn't he? That little blue Catechism the nuns taught me in first grade told us that. He's right here now, isn't he? What's that line, 'when two or three are gathered in my name...'"

"Of course, he is, Joey. Yes, he's everywhere. It's just that going to Mass is special. You remember Holy Communion and all."

"Of course, I do. Still we're not going up there! Wait, I have a better idea. We'll have our own Mass right here!"

"But, Joey, we can't. We don't have a priest. We..."

"What's the big deal, Roz? You always wanted to be a priest and say Mass, didn't you? I know your kind going to Catholic schools with lots of nuns and priests teaching you and you always being jealous you couldn't do what those priests did. So now's your chance."

"No, Joey, it just wouldn't be right."

"You listen to me, you little bitch! Oops, please excuse me! You don't have a choice. We are going to have Mass here and you are going to say it! Or else!"

He touched the point of his knife to the middle of Roz's neck ever so slightly. Just enough to be convincing and for her to feel it against her skin. Then he rattled on. "You have bread and I saw a bottle of wine in the fridge. So we're all set. No, first you need some vestments. Let's see. Oh yeah, you have that real nice robe with flowers all over it hanging in the bathroom. That'll do."

"Dear God, give me strength to go on with this. Tell me what to say. Help me to do the right things. And please, help Joey. He needs you so much," Roz prayed as she took the bottle of wine out of the refrigerator.

When she turned around, Joey was holding out her robe for her to put on. She reluctantly let him help her. "I'll be your server, of course, Father Roz or should I call you Mother Roz? Here we'll clear this table. Only I'll leave the Bible out so we can have some readings. You always need those for Mass."

Roz couldn't believe that she was now standing in the middle of this one room hermitage on a lake wearing her silky pink robe her husband had given her for her last birthday about to pretend to say Mass for this poor man. How did this happen? She never should have left those keys under the leaves on the edge of the shore. Still if Joey had been watching the place as he said, he knew her movements and could have easily overpowered her at any time. She was a proverbial sitting duck on that porch eating her meals or meditating in the rocker or getting ready to go out on the canoe.

And now she was about to say Mass! For all the support she had given the Women's Ordination Conference in D.C. over the years, for all she believed that there would be women priests even within her lifetime, she couldn't believe she was now about to go through with this charade pretending to be a priest by saying Mass for this poor man.

She decided there really was only one thing she could do and that was make the best of the situation. She would "say" the all time best-under-duress "Mass" she could. She knew this was the only way. She started with the words from the beginning of Mass that she remembered so well from her childhood. Words no longer said today but ones she had always loved. She hoped Joey wouldn't notice the discrepancy. "I will go to the Altar of God. To God the joy of my youth."

Joey knelt in quiet attention by the side of the table. Roz continued, her voice tense. "And now let us each examine ourselves for any time we have hurt another person and then ask God's forgiveness. Lord have mercy. Christ have mercy..." She could hear Joey saying the words with her.

"Glory to God in the highest!" she then stated loud and clear.

Joey replied, "And peace on earth to men and women of good will."

"Now for our first reading."

Joey stood up tall and straight beside her, the huge Bible wavering ever so slightly in his hands.

He began, "The first reading is from the last chapter of the Book of Job." Then he started to read selected passages that Roz supposed were significant to him. "All Job's brothers and sisters and former friends came to visit him and feasted with him in his house. They expressed their sympathy and comforted him for all the troubles the Lord had brought on him. Each of them gave him some money and a gold ring. The Lord blessed the last part of Job's life even more than he had blessed the first. Job lived a hundred and forty years after this, long enough to see his grandchildren and great-grandchildren. And then he died at a very great age."

When he finished this reading, Joey heaved a big sigh and sat down on the bed. "Boy, that Job guy really lucked out but not me. Now it's time for the Gospel. Your turn, Mother Roz."

Roz knew as soon as she stood up that she would read some lines from the 16th chapter of Saint John's Gospel. She, too, read only selected parts from the big Bible. Her hands perspired on the page as she recited the words. "You will cry and weep, but the world will be glad; you will be sad, but your sadness will turn into gladness. When a woman is about to give birth, she is sad because her hour of suffering has come; but when the baby is born, she forgets her suffering, because she is happy that a baby has been born into the world."

And then she came to her most treasured lines in all of literature. "You now indeed have sorrow, but I will see you again and your heart shall rejoice and your joy no man shall take from you."

She couldn't help but realize the significant application of these lines to her present situation. She was just about to sit down when she heard Joey remind her, "No, don't forget. You need to do the sermon now, Mother Roz."

Yes, of course, he was right. If this charade was to play itself out well, she had to deliver the homily of her life.

"Brother, in these two readings, one from the Old Testament and one from the New, God is reminding us that He will, in fact, take care of us. He will not let us down. When Job proved himself during all his terrible trials, God rewarded him with material goods, many children and a long life. In a sense throughout his troubles, Job somehow knew with Saint John in today's Gospel, Jesus' words from the Last Supper. That even when we suffer pain, when we have to face sorrow, He will be there for us. He will see us again and our hearts will rejoice and no man shall take that away from us. And so go and live, brother, knowing that God loves you and, no matter what, will take care of you. Do not be sad. He is with you all the days of your life."

Throughout her words Roz watched Joey's head shake up and

down. Her selected readings seemed to be making a real impression on him.

Then like out of a trance, he suddenly stood up, walked over to the table, picked up a piece of the bread and held the glass of the wine in his hands and said, "And this, oh Almighty God, is your body and blood. Not as I live but as you live in me. Amen."

He handed a corner of the bread to Roz and then sipped a bit of wine and passed the glass to her as well. For the next few minutes neither one spoke or moved.

Then out of the corner of her eye, Roz noticed several men soundlessly step up onto the porch. She stayed deathly still.

Joey never stirred even when the men walked into the room. It was as though he was lost somewhere beyond time and space.

Two of the men carefully lifted him up from his seated position on the bed, telling him in very soft, soothing voices, "You're going to be all right. Careful now... Take it easy."

The other man stopped at the door and asked Roz, "He didn't hurt you, did he?"

"No, Ted. He couldn't."

As the men left to go to their car parked up the path by hers, Joey seemed to come out of his trance. Slowly, he turned and smiled at Roz as he said, "You will be sad but your sadness shall be turned into gladness. Your heart shall rejoice and your joy no man shall take from you."

For some reason she didn't quite comprehend Roz felt blessed.

My Dancing Accountant

Paul, my staid, left brained, anal retentive accountant husband rolled out of bed last Tuesday as usual at 8am. He'd been doing that for as long as we've been married and living here in Carmel at the entrance to Big Sur. Something told me that morning that this day was going to be quite different from all the others. I knew my intuition was 99% right.

When I swirled out of bed lazily, oh about a half hour or so later, and ambled to the bathroom, I was sure I heard music downstairs, but Paul never turned on the radio or the TV until 8pm. I crept down the stairs and was nearly knocked to the floor in surprise.

Paul was dancing in his shorts around and around the room to disco music! He seemed possessed, wildly out of character and, as a result, not my husband anymore. Had the mysterious mists from the nearby cliffs off the Pacific Ocean changed him into someone else?

While I wondered, he flicked the radio station and started to do a solo line dance to a country song. Now I was really getting worried. Paul proclaimed a dislike for both disco and country music.

Should I stop him? Turn off the radio? Ask what had happened to him?

Suddenly, it hit me. He was sleep dancing! My dear anal retentive, uptight, left brained, staid man had given it all up for some right brained free flowing fun!

I laughed at this awareness and happily let him dance on!

The Woman in Central Park

Junior Finance Exec. Patrick Kaplan stood stymied in the middle of the Hilton Hotel lobby on the Avenue of the Americas in Manhattan. He had just called his office in Pennsylvania and heard an extremely disturbing message: "Effective immediately, the Scranton, PA office of Bryant, Bryant and Bryant is no longer in business. Please refer all inquiries to our main facility in San Francisco between the hours of 9 and 5 Pacific time."

PK, as his friends called him, recognized the voice delivering the surprising message. It was Bill Smythe's - his office mate's. A young kid just out of grad. school the big boss was grooming for top management although he didn't know it yet. PK had overheard a conversation one evening when he was working late catching up on some back business when "Big Jim" Kantor, the CEO of BB&B, didn't realize he was on the premises.

PK turned toward the bar in the hotel. A bourbon straight up surely would clear his head. Most of all, it might help him figure out what in the hell was really happening at his company. Plopping down on the end bar stool, he ordered his drink as he sat staring at the variety of bottles on the shelves in front of him.

When his drink came, he downed it in two gulps and motioned for another. As he waited for it, his memory tape wound back to the day before when he left his office in Scranton for this three day convention in NYC. Why had his immediate boss insisted he attend this event? Did he want him out of the way to hear of his termination over the phone? Something was not right. What had he missed? How had he been screwed behind his back? Was that kid, his office mate, in on this? Was his being there a set up from the beginning as a spy on the hook of the Big Guys? PK kept asking himself, "Why didn't I realize this if any of it is true?" He felt like he was probably the Biggest Fool of the Century!

When he finished his third bourbon, he paid his tab, left a $10 tip and fled outside for some cool night air. Though a steady rain was now flooding the streets and sidewalks, he walked several blocks then sought shelter under a huge tree at the entrance to Central Park. The rain had sobered him totally. Now he was simply "flippin' angry!" The way he felt when a sure business deal fell through at the last minute or the Stock Market dropped hundreds of points in the last hour of trading. Yes, now he was "flippin' angry!" with no clue what the top brass were up to. How they had obviously set him up to be out of town when the news of his office closure came down. What a God Damned Chump he'd been!

As PK continued to berate himself shaking his head furiously back and forth, his eye caught a woman's as she sat staring at him from a bench nearby. He smiled in spite of himself. She had to be at least ten years younger than he was with shoulder length auburn hair and a svelte body. A quite attractive young woman. What happened next occurred so quickly PK thought he might be dreaming or was still pretty drunk. The woman sauntered over to him, took his hand and pulled him over to the bench to sit down beside her. How could he have resisted? There really was no way. Her smile was contagious.

Peering into his steel blue eyes, the woman said softly, "I know you're in some kind of pain. Maybe I can help you." PK's first instinct was to ask if she was a hooker or if this was an ordinary attempt at a pickup, but something restrained him and he simply replied, "Well, in fact, maybe you can. I need all the help I can get."

"So what's happened? Something serious?"

"I just called my office and found out I'm out of a job!"

PK pounded the back of the bench as the woman shimmied up closer to him. Before he realized what was happening, he felt her arm encircle him. It was so warm and so maternal? No, so friendly, so very friendly. Though he pulled away initially, he threw all caution to the park's beauty at dusk and let himself cry in the stranger's arms for several minutes.

Suddenly without warning he felt her reach for his back pocket and his wallet! Pushing her arm away from his body, he glared at her. "So that's what you're up to! Why I should...." Before he could finished his threat, the woman started to sob herself her whole body shaking violently. PK didn't know what to do. Should he try to console this strange woman who had nearly stolen his wallet and identity?

He gave her his handkerchief as she stared into his blue eyes and asked, "Why didn't you react when I tried to take your wallet?"

"I didn't have a chance. Your crying caught me off guard especially since I didn't know if it was just a show or not. I do have feelings too you know."

"Oh yes, you guys are all full of emotions. Always caring for the downtrodden. Always sympathetic for us women and our problems."

"Yeah. Yeah. So tell me that's the matter with you. Maybe hearing your story will get my mind off my concerns."

"Well, if that's your only motive for listening...."

"So why are you so desperate you have to try to rob me? What's wrong with you?"

"If you really want to know, I was just evicted. I lost my job at a fast food place and couldn't pay rent. Then my super, that dirty old man who only wanted to get to me, became furious when I refused him. He pushed me out the door without even letting me get my stuff. Not that I had that much."

"Come on now, woman, this is the big city but there are laws...."

"You obviously don't get it. Laws mean nothing if you're poor and live one step away from the street and work for less than ten bucks an hour in a shitty job."

The woman began sobbing again. This time PK took her into his arms and let her cry on his shoulder. Anyone watching them would have thought they just made up after a lover's quarrel. They sat in an embrace as the evening street lights flickered on.

When PK stirred finally, he saw that the woman was sound

asleep in his arms. Now what should he do? Or believe? Or think? When he tried to remove her arms from around him, he noticed a ragged scar on her right arm running from her elbow to her wrist. "Who or what caused that?" he wondered. "Was this woman in more of a bad situation than she had indicated?" Though it was quite dark now, fortunately the street light nearby was bright enough for him to also spy a small tattoo of a bleeding heart on her neck.

"Who is this woman? What's her real story? Why did I let myself get involved with her?" PK chided himself. Then he tried again to get her arms off him to no avail. He didn't want to force them off. The only good thing about meeting her was she certainly got his mind off his own problem about his lost position at B, B & B.

The message on the phone came back to him now in a rush as he shifted around on the bench to pull his cell phone from his pocket. He dialed the San Francisco number but only got a busy signal. What was this - a scene in the Theater of the Absurd or what? Grimacing, he dialed his office again hoping the earlier massage was just some bad joke, but no such luck - he only heard Smythe again with the same news that had floored him earlier in the hotel lobby. Refusing to give up, he called the West Coast number once more, but it was still busy.

Now he was "flippin' angrier" than he'd been before and as much as threw the woman's arms off his body. She jumped up yelling at him, "What are you trying to do to me, Mister? Why I should report you...."

"Oh, come on, Lady, remember you came on to me. You and your sad story about being thrown out of your apartment by your horny super."

"Oh no! Did I really tell you that crazy tale? I'm a writer and sometimes I mix up truth and fiction. I've been told I have what are called thin boundaries?"

"I take it that means you have trouble knowing the difference between reality and fantasy."

"So how real are you, whoever you are, becoming increasingly frustrated making phone call after phone call?"

"Sure I am, here I'll prove it." He reached over and pinched the woman hard on her arm. She squealed and nodded, "OK. OK. You're real. I'm real. This isn't a dream."

"Well, it seems like a waking nightmare to me then."

"OK, tell me what's happened to you."

"Either someone's playing a bad joke on me or I've lost my job over the phone by an announcement stating the company I worked for is closed."

"Things like that just don't happen in business, do they?"

"Well, you don't know anything about the real world, do you?"

"Despite what I just told you, I spent ten years working Wall Street playing all the games to keep my position trying as I might to crack through the glass ceiling. Still I've never heard of anyone being let go the way you said."

"If that's true, remember you worked here while I worked in a rather small town absolutely different in every way."

"Pardon me, what do I know? You're making me very upset. Go away!"

"So where are you going to stay tonight?"

"I'll be fine right here. I'll just keep changing benches to stay away from the fuz..."

"No, don't go telling me another one of your stories!"

"OK, then. You go your way. I'll go mine."

PK got up from the bench then and started to walk back to his hotel. By the time he reached the cross walk at the light, the woman was standing beside him asking, "Do have a king sized bed in your room? I can make you forget all your problems."

"So you are a hooker as I originally guessed. I'm not interested and certainly not that desperate!"

They were crossing the street when a horse from the carriage to their right snorted at them. The woman was hanging onto PK's arm. He felt actual desperation from her vibrate into his body. Could she have been telling him the truth in the beginning? Was she homeless with only the clothes on her back and nowhere to lay down her pretty head? How could he find out for sure? Should he go out on a limb and take a chance she really needed his help and his room to sleep?

Though he walked as fast as he could, he made sure she kept up with him. He had to find out how needy she really was. What to say? How to know for sure?

They were within a block of his hotel when she stopped him suddenly by announcing, "All right because you seem like a really nice guy, I'm going to tell you the honest to God truth now."

"So give it to me good, Lady."

"Well, you don't have to get all snooty all of a sudden. I actually don't have a place to stay tonight. An hour of so ago I thought I was really going to have to hang out in Central Park. That is until you came along looking all Brooks Brothers and money so I took my big chance and reached out to you."

"Why don't you have a place to stay? What's your true story? Who are you?"

The woman sighed long and deep, looked into PK's steel blue eyes this time for an extended moment and then blurted out quickly, "I just escaped from a cult in the country up around Albany. I hitchhiked here hoping no one from that crazy group followed me. That's how I ended up in the park. Now, believe it or not, that's the God's honest truth!"

"What kind of cult? How'd they let you leave? How'd you decide to hang out in the park?"

"What is this - the sixth degree? I don't have to tell you every little detail."

"As a matter of fact, you do! I've told you about my own overwhelming day for real, but I still don't know if your latest story is actually true or not. How are you going to prove it is?"

"Well, I don't have a license or any other identification. I took off from the cult grounds on the spur of the moment without thinking I was going to end up so desperate."

"Does that have anything to do with that long scar on your arm?"

"How do you know about that?"

"Couldn't help but notice it while you dozed off in my arms back on the park bench."

"All right then all I'll say is yes. Is that enough?

"No, it definitely isn't! You could be running away from an abusive husband or boyfriend or even a pimp."

"Sure. Sure. I could but I'm not! You have to believe me."

"Why?"

"Just because I'm desperate."

"But that doesn't make any sense. You want me to feel sorry for you like you're some poor little girl all alone in the big city for some unknown reason?"

PK's last words were downed out by a blaring ambulance followed by an even louder fire truck speeding by the two of them as they reached the front of his hotel. The woman was pulling at his sleeve now, "Well, are you going to help me out or not?"

"It has to be not. I'm in a hurry. So long!" To himself he added, "Loser!"

As soon as he got on the elevator for his floor in the high rise hotel, his Better Self plodded him, "What's your problem, Man? What if that woman considered you as her last best hope and you rejected her? How would you feel about yourself then?" PK tossed these thoughts out of his head as he almost jogged to his room at the far end of a long hall. Before he could insert his access card in the door, the woman from Central Park was standing beside him out of breath. Apparently she had followed him into the lobby and somehow found out what floor he was going to.

Elbowing her way into his room, she noted the disarray there. PK remembered then he had left the "Do Not Disturb" sign on the door when he left an eon ago it seemed so he picked up whatever dirty clothes he could quickly and then told the woman to sit on the chair by the window as he demanded, "What do you really want from me whoever you are?"

"At this moment just the use of your facilities if I may." At that she jumped up and flew into his bathroom. PK wondered how long she'd been waiting to relieve herself. She seemed to stay in the room for a long time. Finally, he heard the toilet flush, the sink run and even the shower too. When she opened the door, he was happy to see that she appeared to be less bedraggled and rundown. She had hand combed her now damp hair. Obviously washed her face now all shinny. Even her wrinkled pants and shirt seemed somewhat less of a mess. Most of all, she was smiling a big bright smile. "Oh how I needed that! You are one real Angel Man!"

"Don't get carried away with complements, OK. Remember you as much as pushed your way in here. So of course letting you use my bathroom was the least I could do for such a poor desperate soul like you."

"You got that right. I am desperate. I tried to convince you about my situation back at the park, but you were too wrapped up in all your reservations about me and whether or not I was telling the truth...."

"The deal is, Lady, I still don't know what your honest to God truth is. So why don't you let me in on it once and for all right now!"

"You know what, I would if I could I promise you." She paused looking at the floor and then continued, "The thing is something strange has happened to me maybe yesterday or the day before. I'm not sure."

"How about if you try to put the puzzle pieces together now. You owe me that much."

"For what? For letting me slip into your room? For letting me use your john? For watching you look at me earlier like I was some freak lost in Central Park?"

"Well, weren't you?"

"No! I mean I don't know. That's the honest to God's truth I don't know. Didn't you notice I don't have a purse or anything else. Just the clothes on my back."

"Don't you remember anything? Your name for starters. Where you live. What you do for a living. Where that long scar on your arm came from. The significance of the heart tattoo on your neck. Anything."

"No. No. No. Nothing. Only that I found myself sitting on that bench in the park when you came along. That's all I know."

"Come on, whoever you are, there has to be something you remember."

"I told you I have nothing. Maybe I was hit on the head and all my memories went swoosh as a result!"

"Now you're being totally crazy. Things like that don't happen out of the blue.

"Maybe it was all part of a plan. Maybe I know about or witnessed a major crime. Who did it and all that. Maybe someone tried to erase my memories."

"All I can say to that is you've been watching too much TV - CSI and all those other crime shows."

"No, I don't even watch the tube...Wait...wait maybe...I think I remember something." The women walked past PK and peered out the widow. Then she almost whispered, "They're after me!"

"Who? Who? You don't know, right?"

"Yes, but I think I might have a clue somewhere in my pocket." She pulled out a balled up piece of paper and flattened it out on the top of the desk. When PK looked at it, all he saw was a crayon drawing of a house a five year old might have done. "So what's this mean? What's it tell you?"

"I'm not sure but I think I was in that house... or used to live there... or was kept hostage there or brainwashed there... or saw a crime there... Something...."

"Great! That helped a hell of a lot!"

"I'm trying. I'm really trying." The woman began crying in a crescendo louder and louder. PK hurried to the bathroom for some Kleenex yelling to himself on the way, "This day is only going from bad to worse. Now what?"

When he went back to the room, he was surprised to see the woman curled up on top of the spread on his bed moaning unintelligible words. He covered her body with his robe and sat in the chair by the window hoping when she woke up her mind would be clearer and he'd get some real answers from her.

Falling into a deep sleep in his clothes on the chair, PK dreamed of parks and horses and hotels and crazy women who couldn't tell the truth if their lives depended on it. When he jerked awake as the morning sun shone on his unshaven face, he felt confused and disoriented. "Why am I sleeping here instead of in my God damned bed?" he asked himself sleepily.

Then he heard the toilet flush and he remembered yesterday with a jolt. The weird way he found out he didn't have a job anymore. And the even weirder meeting of the woman now in his bathroom.

"What am I going to do with her?" he asked himself again. Without time for another thought, she exited the bathroom dressed and smiling her big bright smile.

She hugged him and then in a flash was out the door. By the time PK picked up his wallet and access card and charged out of the room, she was gone like an elusive sorceress wielding magic powers. He clamored onto the first down elevator, but he couldn't spy her anywhere in the lobby. Where had she disappeared to so quickly?

He never saw the woman again though he did walk around Central Park some afternoons and evenings for hours on end. Fortunately, though, he did subsequently find out that his office mate had, in fact, played the Joke of His Life on him.

The Candle in the Cathedral

Ignatius Stone, called "Iggy" by his friends, stumbled up the many steep stairs of the Grand Cathedral. Tired. Hungry. Agitated. In the beautiful confines of the huge ornate area of the entrance way, he felt a few blissful moments of peace. A peace that had been eluding him for most of the past year on the other side of the world. A year away from home. A year of joy and pain. Of health and sickness. Of fulfillment and regret.

Moving slowly, he nearly fell into a pew halfway up the main aisle. He tried to breathe deeply to access the peace he yearned to return to his soul. Then after several minutes of intense distress, he was drawn like an unwilling insect to a light in front of the Blessed Virgin's statue in the West Transept. There a double line of votive candles stood flickering in the muted darkness. Mesmerized by their tiny flames, Iggy imagined they were being held in the hands of multiple hypnotists swinging watches in front of his eyes back and forth back and forth....

His presence felt before he came to stand in front of me. Knew his pain. His near despair. His guilt radiating off his body hotter than all my fellow flames combined here on this votive candle table. What to do for him? How assuage his pain? Can my tiny light somehow fight off the guilt radiating to me from his body? I feel at such a loss. So sad for him who has worked so hard for the poor so far away....

Inexplicably, Iggy found himself again swinging up to the top branch of a tree in a dense area of mountainous rainforest in "The Island in the Clouds," otherwise known as Borneo, the third largest island in the world, where he had been doing volunteer work only weeks ago. Searching, always searching for an exotic new healing plant or the bark of a tree that soothed burns or one of the many thousand species of plants that have medicinal qualities. Whatever healing herb he could find to help the people of the Penan, hunter-gatherers of the rainforest, a few of whom were still nomadic. Their way of life has been under attack from the industrialization and westernization of southeast Asia longer than anyone can remember. So many were sick with no energy to forage for food and not enough energy even to eat some days. Their children and older ones were dying daily from malnutrition and disease. He knew if this sorry state of affairs persisted as was likely, the tribe would disappear in a year or two. Maybe sooner.

He thought about the string of what some would call coincidences that brought him here to the middle of the jungle so many thousands of miles away from soft beds, running water and indoor plumbing. All the "taken for granted's" he had grown up with at his parents' home in suburban Northern Virginia. All the "normal" parts of western life that were incomprehensible luxuries here for him and especially for the local population. He rubbed an extremely itchy welt on his arm; he must have been bitten by something or having an adverse reaction to some unfamiliar flora that lived in the trees he was climbing. He had learned from the Penan people that there is a particular insect which can be specially prepared to make an ointment to treat various abrasions, but he never was able to find enough to try it. But he did see flying squirrels and orangutans who built nests in trees instead of sleeping on the ground where wild boar and other creatures would bother them. They built nests to compensate for the fact that without tails they were physically unstable when sleeping in trees.

There had to be some way he could do his part to help these people survive the onslaught of Western Development. It was heartbreaking for him to watch tiny infants shrivel up from lack of nourishment or older people - all of thirty or so - have their teeth fall out of their infected gums. It was unfortunate he didn't have any dental training, but even if he did, what use would it be here? He had no equipment, no medicine, certainly no antibiotics, no... oh what was the use of beating himself up? For their sakes he had to make do. That was all he could do. Make do.

Yes, a number of events had inexplicably led him to these needy people. His science professor in college who recounted stories about the dying group of natives he had heard about here in this jungle. His long-time girlfriend who wanted to be an anthropologist to study those living in far away places like Borneo before she overdosed one night on some prescription pills her doctor gave her. His best high school friend who convinced him to apply for the grant to come to this faraway place to help this poor tribe of dying nomads.

How did all of these apparent coincidences work together to bring him here to this time and place? It was fate or the Will of God or synchronistic events that did it. Right now as he searched the vegetation for a certain exotic plant he knew from his study of botany in college would cure stomach woes, he wished he had a group of students to help him. It was such a daunting challenge to deal with all the dying and try to encourage the barely living to hold on so he could help them survive another day....

☙ ❧

Watching his eyes flicker. Realizing he's reliving his experiences on the other side of the world so many, many miles from his home and civilization. Knowing the pain he's suffered. Is still suffering! May the light of my flame soothe him. May its flickers lull him into at least a momentary respite from his pain and heartache. May my just being here burning right in front of him bring him solace and surcease from the agony vibrating throughout his body....

☙ ❧

Iggy felt a wave of respite as he watched the flames of the candles in the huge cathedral. If it were possible, he would have gladly flowed right into the melting wax around them. But, no, of course, that was ridiculous. He had to make himself face his demons. Make himself stand up to them like a man and a true human being, responsible and caring. One willing to accept the repercussions of his mistakes and frustrations. He bowed his head wanting to pray, but no prayer would come from his soul in near despair. He stood for a long time and watched the flames of the candles flicker and flicker in the muted light of the cathedral....

～ ✍

"Mr. Stone... Mr. Stone... come. Come! The baby.... she need you! You hurry now!"

Iggy ran as fast as he could to keep up with the Penan woman running so very fast way ahead of him. What had happened to this woman's child? How could he help her stay alive? Tears ran down his face as his breath became more and more labored from pushing his legs to run faster and faster and faster....

～ ✍

As Iggy stood mesmerized by the flickering candles in front of him, he felt something strangely soothing emanating from their flames. He didn't comprehend what was happening to him, but he felt calmer and more peaceful now than he had felt in a long time. An extended deep sigh escaped from deep down within his chest as he lowered himself to the marble floor in front of the rows of candles....

～ ✍

I want to do so much for him who has done so much for others. Perhaps my flickering flame will warm his coldness. Will stir him to see clearer. To realize sooner that his decision to leave that other world was the right one. To understand he had done all he could. To lift the guilt holding him down in the depths of depression like a heavy rock. Still he has to find his own way. I can only give him some moments of respite from his pain. Some moments of quiet solitude here in this Grand Cathedral with me. Some few breaths of release from his guilt....

～ ✍

"I'm so sorry.... your baby was very sick. I tried but she's... gone... I couldn't...." Iggy fell down on the dirt floor of the small hut, tears like a mountain stream. He had worked so hard to save the little premature one, but he had failed. And so terribly.

Just as he got up to face the grieving parents, the child moved. Then cried. Actually hardly a whimper but a sign of life nevertheless!

Within seconds the baby's parents were engulfing him in their arms chanting, "She alive! Alive! Savior! Healer! Man of God!" Then the couple fell to their knees in honor at Iggy's feet.

He recoiled at their homage. What did he do? Nothing! He didn't bring the girl back from death. It just happened despite him, but her parents believed otherwise. They believed him to be a healer. A savior. How could he stay in this place honored this way? It wasn't right. It wasn't just. He didn't deserve this adulation. He decided he had no other choice but to leave this place this home he'd shared for many months with these poor Godforsaken people.

A week later he began his long flight back to the states, guilt ridden and sad. Guilt ridden because he left without trying to help others in the area live and maybe one day even prosper. Sad because he really had come to love those kind people....

Oh, poor Ignatius, I wish my flame were a warm hand that could reach out to you. To hold in yours and reassure you that you did all you could in that poor place. You'd made the best decision you could at the time. I will my flickering light to reach out to you in your hour of great need so you will feel whole again soon....

As Iggy now knelt in front of the candles in the cathedral, he could have sworn one shone brighter than all the others. "Are my eyes, my mind, my depression playing tricks on me?" he asked himself. "Surely one candle can't shine that much brighter than the others, can it?" Still no matter how much he reasoned against that possibility, he became convinced that it was true.

In his mind he reached out to that particular candle and felt its warmth like a hand in his as a surge of joy flowed throughout his body. A surge of relief. A surge of peace. He heard words he believed came from that certain candle, "Oh my good man, be of great faith. You have accomplished much in the past year on the other side of the world. And you will go on to accomplish much here as well. Do not give up hope. In time you will feel joy and respite from your pain. Most of all, send love across the world to the people you've helped knowing they will honor the memory of who you were and what you did for them for many generations to come. You are an honorable man, Ignatius Stone. Continue now on your life's journey here at home. Go in peace."

Iggy got up from the floor in front of the candles renewed and peaceful. He couldn't explain it exactly, but he felt as though a dammed up river of guilt had gushed out of his body. He smiled at the candles and then turned and walked out of the cathedral into the rest of his life.

Rose's stories, poems and essays have appeared in the following publications, among others:

Association for the Study of Dreams Newsletter
Burning Light
Dream Network Journal
Futuremics
Ginseng
Ideas Plus of The English Journal
Jungian Literary Criticism
Mad Alley
Networker of the Women Business Owners
   of Montgomery County, Maryland
New Women - New Church
Pablo Lennis
Pittsburgh Mercy
The Critic
The Dana California Literary Society
The Journal of the National Association of Poetry Therapy
The Journal of the National Council of Teachers of English
The Maryland English Journal
The Merton Seasonal

Rosewords YouTube Channel

Featuring HD Book Trailers
and Special Interviews with Rose

http://www.youtube.com/RosewordsBooks

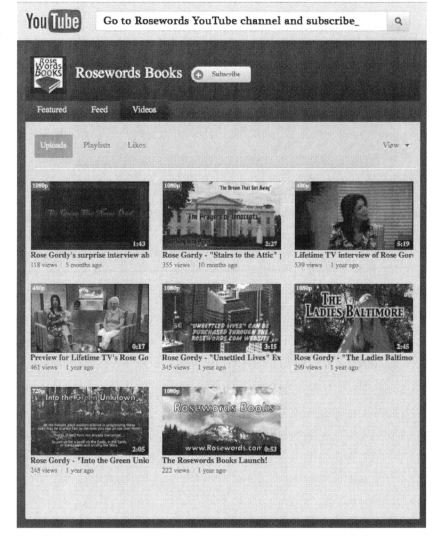

Lifetime Television Welcomed Author Rose Gordy to Hit TV Show The Balancing Act

On June 24th 2011 Lifetime TV interviewed Rose Gordy about her dramatic life and her book "Unsettled Lives"

(Press Release) (Pompano Beach, FL) After the economy crashed in 2008, many people lost their homes and nest eggs, but worst of all they were left with unsettled lives and uncertainty. With the economic crisis ongoing, people are searching for solace, resolution and a new acceptable normal. On June 24th, 2011, The Balancing Act TV show on Lifetime interviewed Rose Gordy about how she has weathered the storm and her new book "Unsettled Lives."

Author and dream counselor Rose Gordy spent thirteen years of her early life as a nun effectively cut off from the "the world of the flesh and the devil." Through her experiences in the convent as well as decades of teaching in the classroom, she has woven a compelling story honoring the lives lost and changed forever by triumph and adversity.

"Unsettled Lives - A Collection of Short Stories" presents numerous tales of people caught in the second-guessing, soul-searching, and uncertain decision-making periods of their lives. In dealing with their lives of quiet and not so quiet desperation, the book's characters may rise above the pain and face new tomorrows with hope and joy. Or perhaps some of them may find their fate in hapless distress and melancholy. What threads of life's twists and turns will determine the direction and destiny that awaits them?

"Having Rose Gordy on 'The Balancing Act' has brought yet another inspiring story of perseverance to women, one that will have a real impact, and help them balance their lives. This is the essence of solutions-based programming, and we're proud that we can bring this to a wide audience."

To view the interview, please visit www.Rosewords.com

What will be found...?

Stairs to the Attic

A Collection of Poems

Expanded
Second Edition

by

Rose Gordy

"Stairs to the Attic - A Collection of Poems" - Available Now in Paperback & Kindle eBook

A sweeping compilation of poems by Rose Gordy illustrating an unusual earthly life relevant to society's oxymorons.

(Press Release) – Rosewords Books is pleased to announce a new book by Rose Gordy. Titled "Stairs to the Attic - A Collection of Poems," this tome is now available for purchase on the Rosewords Books website, www.Rosewords.com. This is the fourth book by Rose of Maryland, following "Into The Green Unknown," "The Ladies Baltimore," and "Unsettled Lives."

"Stairs to the Attic," a book which instinctually eschews the conventional, presents a collection of poetry down to earth yet otherworldly. Amidst the hundreds of little adventures within these pages, readers will no doubt find themselves transported to places and feelings familiar and fantastic. One could watch TV but nothing captures an experience like the timeless rhythmical synergy of song & speech which civilization calls Poetry.

The poem which gives this book its title, Stairs to the Attic, paints a picture of youth restrained but always one step away from the truth. Will a group of ex-nuns find out the secret their convent held from them? What could possibly happen when these liberated women return decades later full of latent curiosity?

Other poems delve into the dreamscape, the synchronistic, the blood bonds, the shadow memories, the earthiness, the maternal instincts, the harkening forward and the eyeful. Filled with 42 original photographs and over 150 poems this unusual book will break the proverbial mold.

"Stairs to the Attic" is available in paperback for $14.99 and can be ordered through the publisher's website: Rosewords.com. ISBN: 1466226269

Unsettled Lives

A Collection of Short Stories

Rose Gordy

"Unsettled Lives" - A Collection of Short Stories - Available Now at Rosewords.com

A wide-ranging collection of short stories delving into the unstrung lives and rattled experiences of modern society.

(Press Release) Rosewords Books is pleased to announce a new book by Rose Gordy and a completely redesigned Rosewords website. Rose's latest book is duly titled "Unsettled Lives - A Collection of Short Stories" and is now available for purchase on the state-of-the-art Rosewords Books website, http://www.Rosewords.com. This is the third book by Rose of Maryland, following "Into The Green Unknown" and "The Ladies Baltimore."

"Unsettled Lives - A Collection of Short Stories" presents numerous tales of people caught in the second-guessing, soul-searching, and uncertain decision-making periods of their lives. Will the myriad characters opt for the "right" path seemingly laid out for them? Yes, they may eventually find their way... but all too often they shall otherwise stumble into unexpected and unique journeys we call the "Human Experience."

Throughout 21 short stories, numerous situations of emotional and social consequence will be offered to the reader. In "Lila, The Love of His Lonely Life," will Charles ever come to grips with his ephemeral obsession? What is Sister Alberta in "Masquerades" aiming to discover by ingenious cloak-and-dagger operations? Furthermore, what could the doctor In "Joy's Esperanza" tell open-minded Joy that would send her into serious self-doubt?

So please join us for psychological jaunts into the various lives within "Unsettled Lives" ... and don't forget to choose the right door in your own.

"Unsettled Lives" is available in paperback for $14.99 and can be ordered through http://www.Rosewords.com.

ISBN: 1456420097

THE LADIES BALTIMORE

Mothers and Daughters
ALONE and Together

Rose Gordy

The Ladies Baltimore: Mothers and Daughters Alone and Together - A New Book

A riveting and sweeping account of several seemingly divergent women in Baltimore, MD.

(Press Release) Author and dream counselor Rose Gordy spent thirteen years of her early life as a nun effectively cut off from the world. In spite of the conditions within the church, she managed to leave and make a life for herself including getting married and having three sons. Through her experiences in the convent as well as decades of teaching in the classroom, she has woven a compelling story honoring the lives lost and changed forever by adversity.

In "The Ladies Baltimore: Mothers and Daughters Alone and Together," an aged nun, a depressed waitress, and a lively teenage girl cross paths on a luncheon cruise in the Baltimore Harbor. Each woman will have a succession of unexpected and unique experiences related to mothers and daughters and to the various men in their lives. Spanning eight decades, the story organically unwinds in non-linear fashion as does life.

But will emotional resistance to the unknown lead them to destroy their vital links to the past? Or will they, through a cascading series of apparently chance encounters and fateful incidences around Baltimore, finally realize how they are profoundly connected? Perhaps time will tell if their lives are sublime results of synchronicity or merely chance encounters.

Also don't forget to visit the avant-garde Rosewords.com website, where you can find the latest on Rose Gordy's books and other projects. Thank you for your curiosity.

"The Ladies Baltimore" is available now in paperback for $14.99 and can be ordered through the publisher's website:
http://www.Rosewords.com   ISBN:978-0-557-418718

Into the Green Unknown
and other Science Fiction Stories
Rose Gordy

"Into the Green Unknown" and Other Science Fiction Stories - Now Available in Paperback

Attention Earth People... Special Announcement about an Interstellar Book by Rose of Maryland

(Press Release) Heralding the release of Rose Gordy's book, "Into the Green Unknown," a collection of 21 science fiction stories and 6 poems, available now at Rosewords.com.

Years in the making, these astounding adventures range from everyday events turned bizarre, to fantastic realms under Earth's oceans, to incredible worlds beyond human perception. Stories such as "The Announcement," "Living Waters At Lucia," and "The Man From Somewhere Else" take readers to strange places they can't possibly journey. Or can they...?

In "Subterfuge," will Madame President be able to protect L.A. from take over by mind-controlling visitors? In "Lost Tides," can two nervous parents protect their children from a celestial disaster and its ramifications? In "The Genetic Casino," will the abducted Ronatta want to discover how she was chosen or remain ignorant and blissful? At the frenetic pace modern science is progressing these tales may be science fact by the time you cast an eye over them. That is, if they have not already transpired....

So join us for a jaunt on the Earth, in the Earth, in the Clouds, and among the Stars.

"Into the Green Unknown" is available now in paperback for only $14.99 and can be ordered at http://www.Rosewords.com. At Rosewords.com you can learn more about Rose Gordy's books and other projects. Bon Voyage!

ISBN: 1456528904

Author **Rose Gordy's e-books are now available on Apple's iBookstore and Amazon's Kindle**

Rosewords Books has released Rose's published tomes for the iPad, iPhone, and Kindle e-Readers

(Press Release) Rosewords Books is pleased to announce the publication of Rose Gordy's four books in electronic book format. With e-book sales now surpassing print book sales on Amazon, the state of the book business is transitioning to a new and exciting era. Accordingly, Rosewords Books now has e-books for sale on Apple's iBookstore, where over 100 million e-books have been sold, and Amazon's Kindle Store, the industry leader in e-book sales.

Before the advent of electronic books, author and dream counselor Rose Gordy spent thirteen years of her early life as a nun effectively cut off from the world. In spite of the conditions within the church, she managed to leave and make a life for herself including getting married and having three sons. Through her experiences in the convent as well as decades of teaching in the classroom, she has written books which honor the lives lost and changed forever by triumph and adversity.

Her four books are titled "Stairs to the Attic," "Unsettled Lives," "The Ladies Baltimore: Mothers and Daughters Alone and Together" and "Into the Green Unknown." All are available at Rosewords.com.

Stop by for a visit

www.Rosewords.com

www.Rosewords.com